SECOND OPINION

Doc Solves Medical Mysteries

Paul M. Gustman M.D.

TABLE OF CONTENTS

ACKNOWLEDGMENTS

First and foremost, my thanks, love and gratitude to my wife and editor in chief Marilyn, for sticking with Doc from first word to last. I believe that by now she can recite the book by heart.

Thanks to Noah Scheiner, our most patient resident artist for the book cover design.

Thanks to our wonderful friends Gail and David Friedman and Suzanne and Marvin Tenenbaum who have served as beta readers, grammarians and who have supported this project in every way possible.

And my immeasurable gratitude to the Medical College of Virginia for teaching Doc, and me, about medicine, how to listen and treat all patients with respect.

CHAPTER 1
CURING AN INFESTATION

Doc sat in the shade of his carport, invisible to those who hurried by. Even if seen he was discounted, leaving no impression more lasting than the hibiscus tree blooming in the warmth of a Tamarac spring. Though unseen, he saw it all but kept it to himself, for rarely would someone stop to chat.

His mind maintained the vitality that his body could not. Sometimes out of boredom and a refusal to watch the talking heads on CNN, he would take stock. As a retired doctor he knew anatomy and physiology well. He knew how the body should work and the myriad of ways his didn't. He would write his own status report starting with the integument, the skin, listing rashes and keratoses, and proceed down from head to feet ending with the tarsal bones—noting the bunion that made his right great toe lose its way and head east when it should be pointed north. The report was initially a test of mental and professional acuity. On a good day it would occupy only twenty minutes and had begun to bore him, even as the list grew over his seventy-six years of life.

He still maintained his medical license, granted each two years. He would complete forty continuing medical education credits on line, obtained from the Cleveland Clinic journal. He would read the articles and answer the multiple choice questions. If he got the wrong answer an explanation appeared listing the reasons he had missed it, and he got another chance to guess until his response was correct. In this way he could get forty hours of credit over a weekend in half the time. Sometimes he had to complete a separate course in prevention of medical errors. This one he liked for it demonstrated how using logic could antici-pate a problem and prevent it entirely. He marveled at the ingenuity of designing anesthesia machines so that the connector for each gas was a different shape, assur-ing that when the anesthesiologist turned the oxygen knob, he got oxygen. There was no practical reason for having a license except to continue the fiction that he was still of use, still had some status in this world.

There were long hours to fill from 8a.m. when his daughter Suzie left to teach her eighth graders and when Marta came to clean up. A stretch of this time was usually spent in the shade of the carport, newspa-per in hand. Some reading went on but he was really observing. He knew that the young guy picking up the trash was having trouble with his right knee. He'd bet it was an old sports-related meniscus tear, not bad enough to sideline him like a ligament rupture would, but painful enough to make him wince when climbing on the back of the truck.

He noticed when the mailman began putting on weight. When he walked by at just the right angle, Doc could see the neck swelling that was a give-away for a thyroid goiter. He had called out to the mailman to elicit a greeting, any words at all, to hear if the man's voice was deeper, making the hypothyroid diagnosis even more likely.

Far more interesting than diagnosing passersby was observing his neighbors. The house next door had been sold several times. The latest owners seemed to have either a large family or lots of friends—friends who would visit at all hours. Their driveway was often full of late model cars. The visitors didn't make a racket, didn't bear any resemblance to the new owners, and came and went quickly. Most were far younger than the age 55 minimum for living in this senior community. None gave him a second glance.

Today's newspaper headline blared, "Opioid Epidemic." It didn't take an epidemiologist to guess that it had moved into his neighborhood. Doc felt secure in his diagnosis. Lab tests were not available for confirmation, unless someone dropped a pill and he sent it for analysis.

He thought about ordering some Narcan in case a visitor OD'ed right outside his door; but he wasn't about to run out and squirt some liquid up a strangers nose for oh so many reasons. His running days were over. He hadn't treated a patient in five years. He didn't want the neighbors to realize their secret was out and that this elderly doctor or his daughter could call the Feds and bring down the flourishing enterprise. This possibility put everyone in danger. What Doc feared most was an altercation in that house, where a stray bullet could easily enter his.

What to do? First he told his daughter.

"Come on Dad, who sells illegal drugs in a senior community. Our folks have so many legitimate aches they get oxycontin prescribed legally."

"But don't you see?" he said. "What better place to hide out than among us. The police won't stake out Tamarac for anything more than over-prescribing mechanical wheel chairs."

"I think you're bored and your imagination is running wild."

"What if there's a shootout?" he asked.

"Oh please! This is Tamarac not Tombstone in the Wild West. You really want to go to the police now?" Smiling a bit, she asked, "If your drug dealers find out you ratted them out, then what?"

"Maybe we should stay with your cousin until this is sorted out."

"Stay with Cindy and her three teenagers? We'd be in more danger of eardrum rupture due to blasting music. Also it would add thirty minutes each way to my commute. I already spend ten percent of my day in a car. Think about it logically Dad. If they are really drug dealers, what would they do if we move out? Would they move in and use our place as a drug den? You've been watching too many episodes of 'Law and Order'."

"Give me a day or two and I'll think of something," Doc mumbled, as Suzie turned on the evening news.

He woke from a fitful sleep with the word 'side effects' in his mind. He was sure his diagnosis was correct, an infection of his neighborhood not unlike lice. His proposed treatments for this infestation did indeed come with side effects. Confront his neighbor and he could wind up in a local landfill. Overly dramatic? Anonymous bodies were forever popping up on the nightly news. Call a professional exterminator: the police or DEA? There was a good chance the neighbors would know who turned them in and might seek revenge. Doc had lived long enough by his estimate. If that was bravery so be it. But not so for his daughter, a school teacher in her prime, or Marta bless her patient soul. If anything ever happened to them, he would wish he had died first.

Eventually he listed the elements of an ideal therapy. The parasites had to leave and not come back. They had to have no reason to suspect his family. A direct call to the authorities would be a last option. Finally a plan began to take form.

Each afternoon, his neighbor would water the mango tree in the front yard. Doc timed the arrival, limped up to the fence on his throbbing hammertoe and said:

"Psssst", and motioned his neighbor near. The elderly doctor kept looking over his shoulder as he whispered to his neighbor:

"You see that house across the street. They must not like me. Maybe they were old patients and thought I did something wrong."

"What makes you say that?" Said the neighbor, himself furtively glancing at the indicated house.

"I see them staring out from behind the blinds, sometimes during the day but even more at night. Maybe they're perverts. See there! They just did it again and scooted away when I saw them."

The neighbor began to sweat as he dropped the watering hose and hurried into his house. Thirty minutes later his garage door opened and a new Mercedes pealed out leaving rubber marks on the driveway.

The next morning Doc was awakened by banging outside. He looked through his front windows to see a realtor pounding a 'For Sale' sign into the soft dirt near the mango tree.

Case closed.

CHAPTER 2
MARTA'S STORY

Doc wore time like a sackcloth. All of the grace and rhythm of his previous life had vanished, as had its purpose. It had been half a decade since he closed his office to "make way for the younger men." The recovery time from a night spent with a sick patient had lengthened from a twenty minute nap to two days. He couldn't deny that even in those last weeks of practice he didn't mind sleep being interrupted. He *actually enjoyed it,* for once he was awake, there was only a single problem to address. There were no casual conversations at 3 am, no one calling for a medication refill or a colleague just wanting to "bounce a problem" off him. He would be totally immersed in solving the medical mystery that was each undiagnosed case; each was a person needing his help. Doc had to admit that he missed it—not dragging through the following day—but the deeply focused hours of being a physician.

He had attended a week long refresher course, coaxing his wheezing steed, a ten year old Camry, to get him to the downtown Marriott on time. Suzie had insisted that he buy a new car with modern crash avoidance technology, but when the salesman addressed all comments to his daughter as if Doc had already begun his passage to the next world, he walked out. "Where are you going Dad?" she asked. "Somewhere where I'm not invisible." he replied.

The medical review course was like a tonic for his bruised ego. He marveled at the newer medications that had sprouted since his retirement, though some judging from the price, must have been planted with a gold plated trowel. He was most interested in the identification of damaged genes responsible for previously undiagnosed syndromes. Medicine seemed to be moving in the right direction—from pure description to identifying causes and perhaps soon enough, correction of the aberrant genetic code, maybe even in utero.

As the spring days sizzled into Tamarac summer, he sat in his carport shade, his fan on high, and read over the course notes memorizing what required remembering. His housekeeper Marta was uncharacteristically late. She parked on the street, or more accurately with three wheels on the street and one on the sidewalk.

"Ay Dios mio. I just lost track of time. I never do that. I'll have to start setting alarms. I'm so sorry Doc. I know I've upset your schedule. I wish I could swear it won't happen again but my brain is on vacation."

"No problem Marta. I'm just doing my homework. Let me walk with you; I have a few questions," he said, holding up his book of notes. "By the way are you on a diet. You look like a shadow of yourself."

"I must be losing, because my clothes are so big. Some hombre malvado stole my hunger. Even when I cook for Jose my stomach does flip flops."

"Have you seen a doctor?"

"Who can afford insurance? It's hard enough keeping a roof over our heads and food on the table. Besides, this will pass. It always has."

"You've had this before?"

"A couple of times, but I thought it was because of the pills for precion alta."

"Oh yes, the diuretics you take for hypertension."

At that moment the front door bell rang and Doc found a scowling Mrs. Greenberg, neck veins bulging. "Your housekeeper just turfed my lawn! Those people should learn how to drive. I wonder if she even has a license," his neighbor nearly shouted the final word as she shook her finger in accusation.

"Did you see her do it?" asked Doc.

"Well I saw her car trench my beautiful grass. With those tinted windows even Superman couldn't see inside. You know how much work it is to seed and fertilize my whole front yard?" she yelled over his shoulder so Marta couldn't help but hear. "Go look! Chunks of my grass are still in her tires."

Doc knew that his neighbor had already called ICE about another housekeeper on the block. He was certain that Marta was legal but was not so sure of the rest of her family.

"I've got a confession to make," said Doc. "My old buggy wouldn't start so I took her car out for a ride to pick up some of that red licorice I love. I don't recall going over your lawn but at seventy-six, I don't remember a lot of things. I'm terribly sorry and of course I'll pay to have new sod put down." He could almost hear the venom drain as the accusers voice reverted to conversational tones and volume.

"I didn't realize it was you Doc. I'm sure it'll be no big deal to fix. I'll just use some of the sand I've got in the garage to fill in. You have a good day," her words in contrast to the lightning bolts hurled from her eyes in Marta's direction.

Marta engulfed in a cloud of shame looked at her feet. "You didn't take my car Doc, but you took the blame. Mil gracias. I don't know what's happening to me."

"You said you've lost your appetite and your stomach hurts when you eat?"

"Yes, I've been eating tums like candy."

"And that makes you feel better?"

"It makes the stomach burning go away, but then nausea comes back worse than ever and I can't remember what I had for breakfast, no recuerdo nada."

"Have you tried going to the University Urgent Care?"

"They wanted $65 before they would let me register and hundreds more after that."

"How about the free clinic?"

"Nothing is free in this country except speech and the rest of the Bill of Rights I had to learn for my citizenship test," she said and managed a smile. "They won't listen to me. They'll think I'm enfermo fingido, a pretender, how do you say it, a crock."

"I'll go with you. Together we'll convince them to get to the bottom of this problem. Let's go in my car. We'll take the long way. If Mrs. Greenberg sees your car passing her house, she may come after us with a broom."

The free clinic looked exactly like what it was, an orphaned space sandwiched between a Dollar store and a payday lender.

The staff, a nurse practitioner and a medical assistant were just finishing a prenatal exam, the older siblings waiting as patiently as three preschoolers could. Marta spoke gently to the children in Spanish and found out about the sister soon to arrive. The mother apologized profusely for any annoyance from her children. "No problema," said Marta.

"Is your grandfather sick?" the nurse practitioner asked Marta.

Doc said: "Marta is the patient and…"

He was cut off: "Well then perhaps I ought to speak with Marta." Doc's face began to redden as if physical blows to his sense of self worth had landed on both cheeks. He reminded himself that this wasn't about him, his ego or his status. The nurse practitioner was very thorough in her history, more so than Doc expected or—he had to admit—than he had witnessed from many of his time pressured colleagues. Doc was ushered from the room during the physical exam, after which the nurse practitioner said: "It's not clear what's causing all your symptoms, but we need to look into this further. It could be diabetes or liver or kidney problems" and to Doc's relief, she wanted to check a CBC, chemistry panel and urinalysis.

"I can't afford this!" cried Marta.

"There is no cost. It's all picked up by the county and private donors." Doc himself had sent extra drug samples to the clinic for years.

"May I make one comment?" said Doc. "I have one other concern. With the GI and neurological symptoms, I was wondering about hypercalcemia especially since symptoms seem to worsen with tums and diuretics."

"You're a medical person? Why didn't you say so? Were you in Family Practice?"

"Internal medicine for forty years if you count residency."

"Well Doctor, no hard feelings; I didn't know."

Then she added: "You know I would have found a high calcium level on the chem panel."

"Of course you would have. I appreciate you seeing this fine lady. I'm just concerned about a parathyroid tumor causing all of this. It would save time and another needle stick if a parathyroid hormone level was also checked along with the very thorough screening tests you've ordered."

"I would like to stop her Tums tablets, which are pure calcium carbonate, if you agree Doctor."

"I do and it would be helpful to stop the diuretics and push fluids while we're waiting for the lab tests to come back. Seems like we'll avoid the invasive procedures for now, but I'm guessing that there is a curative operation in her future.

The next day a stat lab result was relayed to Marta and Doc. "You were right on," said the Nurse Practitioner "and please call me Marcey. We do have an arrangement with the University for emergencies like this one. They reduce or tear up bills completely for our folks. By the way Doctor..."

"Just call me Doc, Marcey, everyone does."

"We could use a physician like you. Malpractice is covered. Daytime hours. You'd be doing a great community service for people who have no alternative. Might give you a challenging reason to get out of bed. Think about it, will you?"

"But I'm seventy-six, haven't wielded a stethoscope for almost five years."

"You've seen a hell of a lot more than I have. There is no substitute for experience."

Doc thanked her for the offer and walked Marta to his car. He lingered at the driver-side door before walking back to the clinic.

"How's Monday" … he said

"And Friday…

To start."

CHAPTER 3

FIRST DAY

Doc awakened at 5:30 a.m., then bathed and dressed robotically in a haze of excitement, anticipation and anxiety, not dissimilar to his first day at med school.

His first thought was to list the tools of his trade that he must not forget today. How would it look if he showed up without his trusty Sprague-Rappaport stethoscope with its two rubber tubes that carry breath sounds more faithfully than any other? Mental note to self: Bring a new copy of The Washington Manual, the intern's bible that got each and every physician through the training years. It had the answers to "What to do till the more experienced doctor arrives."

His second thought was "What the Hell have I gotten myself into? I'm not thirty years old. My reflexes are blunted. When someone came in with uncontrolled hypertension, I used to know the required medication, how much and by what route. Now I'll have to look it up, wasting valuable time." The angel on the other shoulder quickly corrected him. "What if you weren't there? Isn't it better to have an elderly physician who dares to double check, than no physician at all?"

Third thought: OW! As he reached to pick up the newspaper, he met his companions, low back pain and stiffness; one voice saying "How can you possibly bend over patients to examine them?" A voice from the other shoulder answered: "You know this eases up, take a couple of Aleve and keep moving." He recalled a wonderful line from "The Electric Cowboy", a movie where Robert Redford, a rodeo star awakens all twisted and tells Jane Fonda: "The hurt parts take longer to wake up." Right now Doc felt as if he had endured a lifetime of rodeos.

By 6:30 he had eaten his usual breakfast of two hard-boiled egg whites, toast and coffee. He knew that egg yolks didn't raise cholesterol as was believed years ago, one of many reversals of medical "pearls" that were revealed to be plastic knock-offs on closer inspection, but he clung to the comfort of routine.

Next to him was a yellow pad listing the most severe medical emergencies: cardiac arrest, arrhythmias, shock, hypertensive crisis, and anaphylaxis. He then read over the section in the Washington Manual again, more scanning than reading in detail, bringing the facts, the treatments, to the front of the shelf that was his memory.

He was sitting in his car in the clinic parking lot by 8:30, his mind wandering over old cases he could have treated better. He would be smarter this time, or so he prayed. Each wraith of insecurity was decapitated by the good angel before Doc's budding confidence could be undermined. By 8:50 Marcey was tapping a greeting on his window.

"Good morning Doc, ready to face the dragon?" He felt like an actor pretending to be a doctor. He had once read that more than half of all accomplished people felt like charlatans, a group that he now joined. Of a hundred possible answers, many revealing self-doubt, he chose "You bet."

The clinic resembled a railroad car with cinder-block walls. The waiting room with its faux-leather couches, their youth donated to some other office, soon filled with patients. Beyond was the combined file room, receptionists office and pharmacy. There was a scale and vital sign trolley across the hall. Then came two exam rooms staring at each other across the thinly carpeted hall, followed by the doctor's office, now containing two gray metal desks, two chairs and an anemic wobbly book case holding the PDR, repository of current drug prescribing information, a few random textbooks who could not find other homes and a billing manual that was as useful in a free clinic as kindling in a Florida summer. A small alcove, with a school surplus wooden arm chair which documented the love of JR for RB, affection chiseled for posterity, served as their blood drawing station.

Doc was given one exam room as Marcey took the other, he seeing adults, defined as more than sixteen, she, children and prenatal visits. Doc was surprised at how easily he fell into the rhythm of a visit, introducing himself, shaking hands and observing. He sometimes learned more watching a patient walk into a room and climb up to the exam table than with a slew of questions. A patient's ice cold sweaty hand was as good as any psychological screen to indicate anxiety. He believed in listening to how patients answered questions and not just what they said. When he asked a patient "Are you having any chest pain?" and the answer was a waffling drawn out "nooo", he immediately followed with, "What's really happening?"

He lived by the advice of his Dean of Medicine, "Just listen to the patient doctor. He'll tell you what's wrong with him."

The first patient was delighted to meet Doc and immediately began recounting how his grandson, the artist, had just been accepted to RISDI, the Rhode Island School of Design, complete with photographs of his gold key winning paintings. It took Doc a few minutes to realize that the reason for the visit was to renew the blood pressure pills. Prescription in hand Doc escorted the man back to the waiting room where his wife said "I hope he didn't chew your ear off about our grandson. He's so proud."

"Well, lots to be proud of," said Doc with a smile, as he called out the name of the next patient, and the next, each with problems more routine than medically challenging.

The last patient of the day was a thin man who rose slowly, helped by his wife. "Let's go to exam room one." said Doc, as he watched the man's chest rise and his neck muscles tighten with each breath.

"How *OLD* are you?" the man asked, drawing out the word 'old' to three syllables.

"Seventy-six, how old are you?" asked Doc.

"A hell of a lot younger."

"I was too," said Doc," but that was a while ago."

"You still got your license?" persisted the patient as Doc noticed unusual pulsations in his neck veins. "Just renewed last month," said Doc, refusing to take the bait.

"Do they have someone here closer to my age?"

"Well we have a nurse practitioner who is probably half your age; what are you, about mid- fifties?"

"I don't want no kid. I guess I'll settle for you. God, you're even older than old Doc Murphy, who used to come out to the farm before he keeled over at his desk one day."

"Now that that's settled, let's get to know each other. Just call me Doc." And he put out his hand. The patient took it as if he were being offered three day old fish.

"I'm Patrick Boone, no not that one." This was followed by a loud guffaw that soon degenerated into a wheeze, then a cough producing something that was distinctly red on the patient's handkerchief.

Doc just looked at the handkerchief and then at the patient without uttering a word. "I've been doing that for a couple of months, even after I stopped smoking." Doc waited. "And the shortness of breath ain't no better. Comin' in from the parking lot was like a day's work on the farm. The nights are the worst. I have to get up every few hours and can't breathe. Even the asthma puffer I got at the Rite Aid doesn't work anymore. Gotta sit up for an hour soundin' like a steam engine before I can lay back down."

Doc looked at his patient's red flushed cheeks and the slight bluish discoloration of his fingernails.

"Well Mr. Boone"…

"It's Pat, my father was Mr. Boone."

"OK, Pat, were you sickly as a child? Ever have a time when you were kept in bed for a long time?"

"How'd you know that? I missed most of the third grade and couldn't do any chores for months. What's wrong with me Doc?"

"Let me listen to your chest, then we'll talk." Doc heard the wheeze but was more interested in heart sounds. He listened to each individually, first sound, louder than usual, second sound with a wider than normal split, the last part louder indicating high pressure in the right side of his heart. The clincher was a low rumble as the heart relaxed. Doc rolled him onto his left side and the tell-tale murmur became louder.

"Well I don't have all day. Can you tell me now what to do about this asthma."

"I'm not certain, without a few more tests, but I strongly suspect that the illness you had as a child was Rheumatic Fever and it left you with a damaged heart valve which is now making you short of breath."

"What about the coughing up blood? Do I have lung cancer?"

"We'll get a chest x-ray, but I doubt it. Hemoptysis or coughing up blood is often caused by a mitral valve that doesn't open normally. We'll order an ultra-sound picture of your heart valves, an echocardiogram. Would you mind if my colleague, Marcey, listens to your heart? It's not something we hear every day."

"I guess I owe you that, just tell her not to take all day, and she better warm up that damned stethoscope."

The tests were ordered and that Thursday he and Marcey took a call from the cardiologist reading studies at the University. "Well we just made a fascinating diagnosis. Your patient has mitral stenosis. I told him that we would get him better. I sent him to our cardiac surgery team to get his valve replaced."

"You did all this before talking to me, his primary care doctor?" said Doc, making no effort to hide his annoyance.

"Well, the reason I'm calling now is that he's being a bit difficult. He won't see the surgeon until you say it's okay." He and Marcey began to smile in unison.

"I'll call Pat today. I'm sure he'll agree once we talk. And I'm equally sure you'll keep us well informed about his progress and send him back to us for followup."

That night Doc slept well.

CHAPTER 4

THE FUTURE

Doc had avoided nursing homes as if the front door knob would deliver a lethal shock. He had found all manner of excuses not to visit there, though it always left him feeling that he was getting an 'F' on some morality quiz. The first building with its piano in the main lobby and 4 p.m. ice cream socials was barely tolerable. Building two, for those in need of metallic assistance, the walker and wheelchair brigade, was tougher. Building three, for those who needed assistance to perform the most basic of bodily activities, was avoided like a dose of castor oil.

How had he agreed to this?

"After seventy-six summers I should know what I can tolerate and what makes me shudder," he muttered to himself just as Marcey interrupted with:

"Thanks for filling in Doc. Dr. Stein says he'll be back next week, so this should be a onetime gig. He has thirty-two patients, most in building three. They're pretty stable. We don't anticipate that any will be going by red light to the nearest ER."

"Are you OK, Doc? You look a little far away."

"Just thinking about the last two weeks at the clinic. You were right; I do look forward to coming there. This place, however, is not on my wish list."

They took the first chart rack and headed down the hallway. It was accessible only with an electronic pass, not unlike a credit card, touched to the entry switch. The doors swung open for exactly thirty seconds, then closed and locked behind them with an undeniable click, joining the healers and patients in medical incarceration. Doc understood that the locked doors were necessary to discourage wanderers; though being unable to leave was a feeling that took some getting used to. The nursing cart was down the hall—full to overflowing with patient meds, bandages and the defibrillator that hung on one side: a particularly harsh intervention reserved for those without the magic letters, DNR, do not resuscitate, on the front page of their chart.

Bed One held an elderly woman who greeted Doc with a huge smile.

"Look at you," she elated, "Not a little boy anymore! So good to see you. Don't you look handsome," as she clasped her hands in front as if offering a prayer of thanks.

"Hello Mrs. Graham, I'm just helping out your doctor for today."

"Of course you are. So good to see you. Not a little boy anymore."

"How is your breathing, It says you had some shortness of breath last night."

"Oh I'm fine, fine and dandy."

"I see your legs are swollen."

"Are they? I wonder when that happened."

"What do you think Marcey?"

"The chart says she had a heart problem that made some fluid back up into her lungs, congestive heart failure. Looks like that may be happening again. I suggest we restart her water pills and put her on a two gram sodium diet."

"That should get you feeling better Mrs. Graham," said Marcey.

"You're so nice," she said, squeezing Marcey's hand.

Room Two smelled of urine and decay. "This is Mr. Duggan who was transferred here from the hospital when his Medicare days ran out. There was a discharge note as well as a DNR sheet on the front of his chart signed months ago by a Mrs. Rossin, from Los Angeles, apparently his nearest relative. He has decubitus ulcers that have been debrided multiple times. He's a metabolic mess, with all of his organ systems barely hanging on. He doesn't get out of bed without maximal help." Doc noted the lack of social history other than an absence of smoking or drinking.

The same was true of the next few patients. All were grey in hair and spirit. All were on the far shores of life and didn't recognize the tsunami that was coming, or didn't care or would welcome it. The nurses helped roll the patients on their sides to point out the abrasions that would soon be decubitus ulcers despite the patient being turned every two hours. Doc prescribed creams and a special air mattress to ease the consequences of immobility. Most rooms had the same pastoral scenes painted at some commercial art mill in a far off land. Most had no personal photos, nor did the nurses' notes reveal family who made more than perfunctory visits if papers needed to be signed.

After a couple of hours they finished rounds. "Do you want to get some coffee?" asked Marcey. Doc agreed though his every instinct was to flee. "Pretty depressing, isn't it," said Marcey.

"You have no idea, especially when you get to my age. One blood vessel blocked and I'm in building three. Worst of all, is the anonymity. I look at Mr. Duggan and ask 'Who were you'? He could have been a titan of industry or a janitor, a true believer or an agnostic, could have come from Manhattan or a farm in Tennessee. It's the loss of identity that I find most disturbing."

"That will never happen to you, Doc. You'll always have your patients who will remember you… and you'll have me."

"Thanks Marcey. That means more than I can say. Let's just hope Dr. Stein stays healthy so I can keep creating memories at the clinic, even if we don't have 4 p.m. ice cream socials."

CHAPTER 5

DOC TAKES A SICK DAY

Clinic days went quickly. It was hard to believe the arms of his watch weren't being manipulated. He started at 9 a.m., after having had his morning coffee and read his newspaper at home. He blinked twice, or so it seemed, and it was lunch break. If asked how much time he spent with each patient, Doc would say "enough." Was this unnoticed acceleration of the clock a good thing? He felt a satisfied fatigue at day's end that he had not felt in years, as if he had just rowed across the finish line of a long, hard race.

That was answer enough.

Suzie was worried that he was taking on too much, now that his clinic hours expanded to three days a week plus that odd day at the nursing home. She kept reminding him that he had to respect the accumulated decades and give them their due.

"What exactly does that mean?" he asked. "Should I sit bundled in a knit blanket and not venture out? Come on Suzie, I'm sleeping better than ever; the back pain has not been an issue. I look forward to going to work. I like the simplicity of that clinic. We see all comers and there is no worry about their ability to pay for tests or if they can afford the drugs."

"I'm just worried you'll catch something, especially from the little kids in the waiting room. It's viral quicksand waiting to suck you in."

"You know Marcey sees the little ones, but you do have a point. Maybe we can partition the waiting room into one area for sick kids and the other for everyone else. Even a curtain would help. As for me, I'm of the school that depends on Ivory Soap and water. I wash so often my skin is beginning to crack. I've had my flu shot, the high dose one. I have patients wear masks if they are coughing or sneezing when they hit the door. It's been three months and the foul bugs haven't found me yet. Besides, working Monday, Wednesday and Friday I have a day to rest after each clinic marathon; no, make that after each clinic wrestling match between the evil forces of disease and the good guys."

It was a typical Friday clinic, busy for Marcey with the Moms who wanted to get their sick kids seen before the weekend, and for Doc, seeing those adults with the same motivation. The waiting room had been curtained off but Doc didn't really believe that would have a major effect upon infection control. At least the little ones weren't coughing and sneezing directly upon those of his patients who were frail and elderly.

Just as they were closing up shop for the weekend a car parked outside and a lady knocked vigorously: "Am I too late? Oh God I hope I'm not too late, please help me."

"Come in. What's wrong?" asked Doc.

"It's not me, it's my husband, he's still in the car but he needs help getting inside." Marcey brought out the wheel chair and delivered an obviously ill appearing man in his seventies to Doc's exam room. He was coughing and appeared to be short of breath.

His vital signs confirmed a fever of 100.5 degrees and an elevated respiratory rate of 22. Doc noted that his neck muscles did not contract with each breath nor did his nasal openings flare with air intake. Those signs would have meant respiratory compromise that would have led to a red light ambulance to the ER.

Doc introduced himself, and began with "When did all this start?"

"I've been coughing and have a fever and sweats at night. I feel like hell." After Doc determined that this had been going on for more than a week, that the patient was not coughing anything up, had no chest pain, had not been eating well and had lost a couple of pounds, Doc asked him to remove his shirt and listened carefully to the whole circumference of his chest. In the right upper chest, just below the clavicle Doc heard tell-tale crackles, not unlike the sound of Velcro opening. This usually meant pneumonia, so Doc, with Marcey's help, did a chest x-ray. The machine could have been the prototype developed by Roentgen in 1896, but with the help of some very smelly developing fluid, it produced serviceable pictures. Doc could see the lacy infiltrate in the right upper lobe from across the room.

"You've got pneumonia, Mr. Johnson. Let me ask a couple of questions more.

Have you traveled recently?…….. "NO"

Have you been on a farm recently?….. "NO"

Have any pets?…… "NO"

Ever had a TB test or any form of lung disease in the past?"……………….. "NO"

What kind of work have you done?" When no clues could be squeezed from the patient, Doc spoke to Mr. and Mrs. Johnson. "You clearly have pneumonia, and I think you should be in the hospital to find out what's causing it and get you on the right medication."

The couple exchanged a look that Doc couldn't immediately translate before the patient said:

"No way in Hell am I going to that death trap. My brother-in-law went in with a sore leg and wound up dying of blood clots to his lung. If I'm going to die, I'll do it in my own bed, thank you."

"But there are all kinds of tests they can do in a hospital that I can't here."

"Which part of 'no way' did I not make clear?"

"Well the best I can do is to start you on an antibiotic pill that will be effective for many types of bacteria, but not all. I'll put on a TB skin test, but we have no sputum to culture, so we're at a distinct disadvantage. In the hospit ..."

"NO!" Shouted the patient as he ripped off the mask and dissolved in a spasm of cough in Doc's direction. Doc gave Mrs. Johnson his home phone number and told her to call over the weekend if she had any questions. Both knew his answer would be "go to the ER." Both knew that advice would be roundly ignored. The patient was to return first thing Monday morning.

Doc waited all weekend for the phone to ring, but it never did. Come Monday morning there was Mr. Johnson looking notably worse. Doc could see that his neck muscles were contracting with each breath. "Those antibiotics didn't do a thing," he said. "My temp is 101 even when I take Tylenol. And I'm coughing more than ever."

"How about your breathing?"

"Going to the bathroom is all I can manage. Sometimes I barely make it there and the breathing is so hard I have to wait a few minutes before going back to bed."

"Mr. Johnson, before I waste your time and mine going through our previous discussion, let me point out that right now you are a public health hazard, a danger to your wife, kids and grandkids. Even though the skin test is negative you could have TB, or some other highly contagious disease. We tried your way of outpatient treatment and it's not working. You need to go to the hospital for the sake of those around you, for your grandkids, if not just for yourself. How would you feel if one of them died because of a treatable disease that could have been diagnosed in the hospital? Why don't you two talk it over?"

"You can stay Doc," said Mrs. Johnson. Turning to her husband she said, "I'm scared George, for you and for the baby. You were near her when you started coughing. If something happened to that child because of what we did, or didn't do, I couldn't live with myself." Doc quietly exited the room. A few minutes later the door opened and Mrs. Johnson said but two words:" He'll go." The ambulance came quickly and despite his protests, Mr. Johnson left the clinic on a gurney with oxygen in his nose.

Doc sent a written summary of his history, physical, x-ray findings and impression along with his phone number and a request to be informed of the patient's progress. By the end of the day, Doc could wait no longer and he called the hospital, immediately entering the fast track when he identified himself by the title Doctor. The special physician's operator located the patient, now in the ICU and the intensivist on call came to the phone. They were preparing to intubate Mr. Johnson, who was having more trouble breathing. This would also give access to remove secretions which could help identify the culprit, the cause of this illness. Doc's shoulders sank in sympathy and sadness.

The next morning, Doc noted a message on his phone. It was Mrs. Johnson. "There is one thing I forgot to mention."

Just then Doc began to cough.

CHAPTER 6

DOCTOR AS PATIENT

Doc began to sweat. Marcey noticed and said, "Let me take a look at you, if that's OK."

"I would appreciate it," said Doc.

"You've got a mildly elevated temp. Doc, it's 99.6. You're a bit flushed and you are sweating. I'm hearing a few scattered crackles in your chest, so this could be the start of a lung infection. Let's pretend it's not you. With another man of your age with an elevated temp. and an abnormal exam, it would be malpractice if I didn't send you to the ER."

"What about a chest x-ray here?"

"Now you're beginning to sound like Mr. Johnson. You know the quality of the hospital's digitized x-rays are better than those we have here. Besides they'll have a real radiologist reading them. Come on, I'll drive you over. We can contact your daughter on the way."

"She's going to rake me over the coals about catching something here, which is what she feared all along."

"The only safe way to live is in a bubble, and that's no fun at all," said Marcey.

She noted that the ER registration for an insured doctor was a breeze compared with trying to get an uninsured patient evaluated. Doc presented the big three: his Medicare card, AARP secondary insurance card and his driver's license. He was taken to the 'back' and placed on a stretcher in an isolation room. Apparently the room vented outdoors and air pressure was adjusted so that air would not be shared with surrounding rooms.

In rapid succession Doc met the nurse, the nurse practitioner, the x-ray tech, the phlebotomist and finally the ER doctor, who said, "Not so much fun on that side of the stethoscope, is it?" Doc smiled, and couldn't disagree.

"You're pretty efficient here," said Doc.

"We have an algorithm for treating most diseases, and the one for pneumonia demands ninety minutes or less from when you hit the registration desk to when you get your first dose of antibiotics." As if on cue the nurse came in with a small bag of light orange colored fluid and hooked it into the newly placed IV. "That's a broad spectrum antibiotic that should kill most of the common bacteria causing pneumonia. Marcey's diagnosis was correct," said the ER doctor.

"You can see the start of an infiltrate here," he said pointing to the image pulled up on the screen of one the ubiquitous computer carts.

"What happened to paper charts?" Doc said out loud.

"I miss them too," said the ER physician, "but you can't fight progress, if that's what this is. We'll get you admitted as soon as a bed is available upstairs. If all goes well you should be home in a couple of days."

Suzie then came through the door looking ready for combat. She could not have appeared more formidable had she carried a broadsword and been bedecked in armor. No one was foolish enough to stop her charge as she made it to Doc's stretcher.

"Are you OK? I knew something like this would happen. Are they going to keep you?" All tumbled out without leaving space for anyone to cut into her verbal rush hour traffic. Finally she took a breath. The ER doctor introduced himself and gave a one sentence summary, unsure if he would be allowed to go further. "Your dad has pneumonia and we've started him on an antibiotic." When Suzie didn't jump in, the doctor went on. "We're not sure of the causative organism, and we think he ought to be admitted for a couple of days until we're sure he's on the mend."

The cork popped as Suzie blurted out, "That clinic!" and could go no further as her face reddened. Doc interjected, "We'll talk about that later," and the door could be heard closing on that issue…for now.

By the next morning he was worse. Temp was 100.8 and he had some chills. He felt as if all his energy had been siphoned out during the night. Suzie saw it immediately, and had a call into the hospitalist, the in-house physician who had admitted Doc. She was anxious but more composed than the previous evening. It was a school workshop day so she was not being torn between two destinations. For better or worse, Doc had her undivided attention.

After the usual debriefing, Doc asked her, "And how are you doing with all this? I know I didn't sleep well with all the interruptions for vital signs and IV bag changes. How about you?"

"Well there was one thing. Each time I closed my eyes the phone rang. It was Mrs. Johnson. She said it might be important. I have no idea what that means."

"Oh my goodness, I forgot all about Mr. Johnson. Give me a second to call up to the ICU. Then I can give his wife an update, which is probably why she is calling." The head nurse told Doc that Mr. Johnson was unchanged and still critical, Smears for TB were negative; fever persists, still on a mechanical ventilator, now requiring 50% oxygen which means the lung function is slightly worse.

Doc sighed and picked up the phone to call. Suzie interrupted him. "This is crazy Dad. The clinic put you here and will put you in your grave if you don't rest up. You're the patient now. Remember 'Doctor heal thyself.'"

"I'm too tired to fight with you Suzie. I just need to close my eyes."

The next thing Doc knew it was two hours later and a nurse was waking him for vital signs. "There is a lady outside who has been waiting to see you. She says her name is Mrs. Johnson." Suzie popped up from her corner chair like a jack-in-the-box. "No way."

"Oh come on," said Doc. "I never called her back and her husband is so sick."

"So is her husband's doctor!" countered Suzie.

"Just a couple of minutes, no more, I promise." When did we trade parental roles? Doc wondered.

Mrs. Johnson wore her worries on her furrowed brow. "I'm really not stalking you Doc. I'm so sorry you're sick and I'm afraid you and George may have the same thing." Suzie was starting to get out of her chair to end the visit, a move Mrs. Johnson seemed to anticipate. She blurted out: "Remember when you asked George if he had any pets?"

"And he said no," Doc replied.

"Well he doesn't have any pets because his parrot died, about two weeks ago."

"That's it!" cried Doc. "That's why George is not getting better on the usual antibiotics. I've got to talk to his doctor immediately." Doc reached the intensive care specialist on duty and said," Mr. Johnson most likely has Psittacosis, parrot fever. It would be great if you could order blood for antibodies against the causative organism and start him on tetracycline ASAP. Doc repeated the same conversation with his own doctor who ordered tetracycline, a drug he rarely used.

"I must apologize, Mrs. J," said Doc. "You've done everything but break into my home to give us the key piece of information and I wasn't even smart enough to call you back."

"I think you had a couple of things on your plate, and still you found time to see me today."

"By the way, I think you just saved your husband's life." A sob welled up from her pool of barely suppressed fear and relief.

Three days later Doc was discharged. He didn't ask the dietician for a single recipe.

Suzie knew her battle was lost after Doc's first sentence: "You can't hide from life, my love; it may be safer, but it's not living." She did get him to wait until after the weekend before going back to the clinic. When he did return, Marcey had a chocolate cake, his favorite, topped by a bottle of tetracycline.

CHAPTER 7
SERPENTINE

Doc looked forward to the morning NY Times. He always read beyond the headlines because the really memorable details were more often found on the page five continuations. He loved the op-eds. He also took a crack at the crossword puzzle which Suzie had to finish especially after Thursday, when the tricks started—words wrapping around, multiple letters in each box and other evils of the Puzzle Master's trade.

For the past two days the paper was not there. Today was the Sunday edition which he really missed. That crossword had a clue that once diagnosed, opened up the rest of the puzzle. The week in review, and the book review sections were among his favorites, and among the missing. Occasional papers had gone AWOL in the past but not three out of four days. He placed the problem into a medical algorithm.

Symptom: Missing Newspaper

Duration: New onset, thus acute, or sub-acute at worst.

Etiology—Unknown

Differential diagnosis—

1. Must rule out a delivery problem, maybe the newspaper never made it to the door, or was delivered to the wrong house.
2. Maybe it was delivered properly but not in the usual place, in the hedges or under the car.
3. Maybe it was delivered and someone took it. Doc knew how awful it was to accuse someone wrongfully. The delivery man? He could lose his job and it might not be his fault. A neighbor: this could create a feud of monumental proportion ending with problems for Marta or sacrificing the peace of the neighborhood.

This situation might require some delicacy, thought Doc.

"Let's try a simple approach first," he thought. Doc set an alarm for 6 a.m. and was outside just as the first rays of sunrise began to paint the cloudy canvas in pinks and flamingo orange. No newspaper. He looked in the hedges and even managed to bend down on hands and knees to look under the car. No newspaper. Getting up was not so easy.

He was not about to wake up and wait outside at 4:30 a.m. to speak with the delivery man, but Doc did get the name and phone number from the newspaper, being careful to say there was no problem, just that he owed the man a Christmas present. The deliverer assured Doc that he had been on the same route for three years and had never missed a day, not even when there was a hurricane watch. He obviously took great pride in his work, and Doc felt a pang of guilt just raising the possibility of malfeasance. "I never miss a day, never," he repeated.

Doc needed a diagnostic test. X-rays and MRI's seemed inappropriate for the current dysfunction. How about another set of eyes, that could see in the dark? Doc was surprised to discover that there were such things as 'spy shops' and that one was in his local mall. The owner looked like Mickey Spillane going to seed. His arms were still big, but not as big as his belt line. He had acne which in someone his age suggested steroid usage. He used to be a private detective, he said, but no longer had his license for reasons he chose not to discuss. Doc felt he was in a wonderland for the nefarious set as he went from one glass case to another.

There were baseball hats with hidden cameras, for $49.95; he didn't wear a hat. Water bottle cameras cost $79.95; he didn't carry the mandatory South Florida water bottle. There were cigarette lighter cameras for $84.99; he didn't smoke and never had. And there were cameras hidden in smoke detectors for $69.99.

Doc finally settled for a motion activated camera that looked like an AC adaptor and could be plugged into his carport outlet having a view of the newspaper landing area. Doc thought more than once about the $69.99 price compared with the cost of replacing a few papers. It came down to the principle, the violation of his property, and even more was his curiosity to discover the culprit, to make a diagnosis.

The first night the camera must have been angled incorrectly for Doc saw a shadow, but only a shadow, and his paper was gone. That afternoon he pretended to place a book on a shelf but actually turned the camera thirty degrees to the left. The next day he awakened, and was embarrassed by how excited he was to see the recording. Out of the dark came a figure that he recognized even before seeing a frontal view. It was unmistakably Mrs. Greenberg who bent and then scooped up the blue double bagged newspaper and nearly sprinted away.

Gotcha! Thought Doc, and I imagined this private detective work was harder than medicine. But what to do now? Confront her and she might make a scene that could last for years. He would never go to the police, but even if he did she might be vindictive and take it out on Marta with an anonymous call to ICE.

Doc thought and thought. What had she said when they spoke shortly after the Greenbergs moved in? It was just on the edge of memory. Two days later he awakened with a clear recall of the conversation and a plan. Doc took the old, old Camry out for a ride and "No, Marta," he didn't need company. He came back with a strange grin that Marta had not seen before.

The next morning he was awakened with a scream from outside their car port. Doc didn't move from his bed. He reviewed the conversation he had with Mrs. Greenberg shortly after she moved in. "Oh the weather's nice alright, if you don't count summer. And the hurricanes were a constant threat, but the worst of all were the snakes." Oh she hated the snakes. They made her skin crawl.

It wasn't hard for Doc to find a pet shop in town. Black racers were popular pets. One could fit in a plastic bag next to an old newspaper Doc had saved. A single call to the deliveryman had ensured that today's paper would not be delivered, and only the one holding the 'gift package' would adorn the carport.

His newspaper was scattered along several lawns as was one sandal. The black racer was never found, and as if by magic, the newspapers showed up every single day.

CHAPTER 8

IT

Doc introduced himself to the patient in his usual way despite the new presence in the crowded exam room. It was a metal cart on wheels, supporting a computer screen and keyboard. Doc tried his best to ignore the intruder as he watched the forty year old patient climb onto the exam table like someone decades older. "How can I help you?" was the usual first question.

"I have sores on my legs that won't go away, and I'm puffing with any exertion, and my eyes burn and are red. It makes no sense to me. I didn't hit my legs on anything that I remember."

"How long have you had this?"

"A couple of months and hey, aren't you supposed to enter all this in the computer."

Doc enjoyed the clinic with one notable exception, the computerized records. They had switched to a New-Gen system at the Board's request. The local hospital had installed it for free and threw in two computer trolleys that could be wheeled from room to room. Their main selling point was that all hospital data including x-rays and lab results could be accessed from the clinic without endless phone calls. The main incentive for the hospital was a government grant that would pay thousands of dollars for each office that adopted EMR—Electronic Medical Records. The total amount would pay for all the hardware and software, with some left over for an ER expansion.

"Are your joints swollen?"

"Just a little, but my knees hurt going up stairs."

"How bad is the pain, from 1-10?"

"Maybe 2 out of 10. And I have no appetite."

"Anyone else sick at home?"

"I'm the only "lucky" one. You know, at the hospital, the doctors never look at me, just at those damned screens. You're the first one who could identify me after a visit."

"When were you at the hospital? Did they do any tests?"

"Last week, at their walk-in clinic, they did some basic blood work, but I told them no more tests when they told me what I'd owe for it; and I mean 'owe' since I can't pay those retail prices. Do you know that if you have no insurance they charge you MORE. Unbelievable!"

There had been several computer lessons that Doc and Marcey had attended and eventually a 'go live' date when all records, medication orders, and lab tests marched to the commands of New-Gen. Both Doc and Marcey wrestled with the system, though it seemed much easier for the younger woman. They both kept trying to fit the computer into their normal work flow. Somehow there was always one more step they hadn't anticipated. It seemed that they were being forced to alter their smooth routine to accommodate the demands of a rigid software program.

They could type prescriptions into the computer which would simultaneously become part of the medical record and be sent instantaneously to the patient's pharmacy. The problem was, looking up the correct pharmacy required going down a multi-page list of all the CVS pharmacies in South Florida. Doc tried once, then twice and eventually just wrote out the prescription by hand.

And the letters to other medical facilities were maddening. The computers were programmed to use certain phrases derived from check off lists that never seemed to emphasize the exact point Doc needed to make. There may have been a place to note wheezing, but not the more ominous combination of wheezing plus decreased breath sounds, indicating very severe asthma, which was never clearly expressed in computer-speak.

Doc disliked the presence of a third entity, the computer, in the exam room. This meant he would be looking at the computer while asking questions and not at the person opposite him. It was like examining the patient with a blindfold on. How could he judge the quality of the answers to his questions if he was staring at a computer screen and didn't watch the non-verbal clues, the smile, the grimace, the look of uncertainty? The solution that both he and Marcey eventually found was to jot down a few notes during the visit and then do computer entry at the end of the day. This added at least an hour to each workday. He was told that many physicians, especially those in higher paying specialties, employed scribes. They would do the computer entry before the doctor even entered the room. At times this resulted in a completed chart even before the doctor met the patient—a situation that to Doc, emitted the rancid odor of dishonesty.

He noted the raised red areas on the patient's shins. So this was a disease that was affecting multiple organ systems, the skin, and from the history of shortness of breath, probably the lungs as well.

Doc entered the patient's social security number, wondering why on earth that most valuable piece of our financial identity was used to access medical information. The patient's file popped up. Pushing on the 'Laboratory Tests" tab made the screen light up with many red blinking lights. Most prominent were the liver function studies, each one abnormal. His red and white cells were mildly decreased. Doc added liver and bone marrow to his list of affected organ systems.

There was one New-Gen feature, a throw in, that Doc found fascinating. Included in the programming was Pub-Med, a search of the NIH archives, a computer sorted library of medical literature covering all diseases common and obscure. At the end of each day, Doc would look up the current literature on a new drug, or an old disease. He never failed to pick up useful information.

He excused himself and rolled the computer cart to his office. He typed in, 'Pub Med' and was led to the NIH website. He typed into the box with the magnifying glass, just as they had shown him: 'multisystem disease'. He narrowed the search by typing 'review articles' into the 'filter' box. Up popped a list of medical curiosities. There was Lupus, the strange autoimmune disorder where the body attacks its own organs with toxic antibodies. There were all manner of strange infections, relatives of tuberculosis that spread far from the lungs. At the bottom of the page was a name he had not thought about for quite a while, but one that fit the current picture well, Sarcoidosis.

"I have a pretty good idea of what's wrong with you thanks to this electronic assistant. It's called Sarcoidosis, a disease of unknown cause that affects some or all of the organ systems, especially the liver and lung. And it is easy to prove."

"I never heard of this. Is it new?"

"Lots of cases were found in army recruits when chest x-rays became part of routine induction physicals.

A highly suggestive finding on a simple chest x-ray is lymph node enlargement. It's easy to spot so I'd like to do one now." This was done and Doc and Marcey found just what they were looking for.

"We would like to have a conjunctival biopsy done to prove the diagnosis. Our ophthalmologist will numb up the red area that collects tears below your eye. It's painless and by far the easiest way to confirm the diagnosis."

"Is there any treatment?"

"Many people don't need any medication, but with the skin lesions on your legs and the abnormal liver functions, I think a trial of prednisone would make you feel better quickly."

"Still here?" said Marcey as Doc finished dictating a letter to the hospital for their records. He didn't love the computer program which kept him past 6 p.m., but he did have respect for his new rigid colleague.

CHAPTER 9
FRIENDS

Doc had gone to too many funerals of late. He had eulogized Sam, his lifelong friend, the cheerful pharmacist who could make the challenges of old age into a hilarious punch line. He was so much fun that Doc would sometimes ride along while his friend played "geriatric golf." Sam was tired of being denigrated by the immovable score card where par was arbitrarily set to reflect the skill of a twenty something, so he invented "senior par", a new scoring system that raised the expected standard by one stroke per hole for those over 70 and two strokes for those over 80. He was tweaking the system to make allowances for joint replacements when he fell forward one day with a fatal cardiac arrhythmia, a 'coward's end' as Sam had always labeled it. Doc still felt guilty that he was not there at the moment his friend needed him most.

Other friends and acquaintances had moved to be near their children, even if that meant braving Chicago winters, or Phoenix summers. Knowing that their parents were nearby provided a sense of well being to parents and children alike. The clinic had become Doc's new friend. He loved it for many reasons. There was the comfort of routine, the occasional challenge, the sense of accomplishment. He loved the human interaction, getting to know his patients as people, not just medical 'cases'. Doc liked one couple in particular, Bill and Helen Gordon. They had been Marcey's neighbors and came to the clinic because they liked her and by extension, Doc. They had Medicare coverage and a supplementary policy through their NY teacher's retirement plan. They were two of a very small population of clinic patients who paid full freight and were glad to do it.

Doc looked forward to their visits, using those opportunities to catch up on their grandson's high school basketball career and to which college their granddaughter, the artist, would apply. There was the official business, renewing prescriptions, ordering blood tests, then came the fun part. Theater, movies, or the latest Miami Heat roster were all fair game. Like most people Doc had met in Florida, they avoided the taboo topics of politics and religion. Doc appreciated not being lectured, as he was by the few zealots in his practice. His own beliefs on most subjects had been tempered by the years. There were very few absolutes, rights and wrongs, blacks and whites. His was now a sepia universe.

The Gordons enjoyed Doc's company and especially the fact that he remembered their grandchildren's names. They did not know that Doc, who was afraid that his memory might fail him one day, had typed the grandkids' names and interests on the front of the EMR, the electronic medical record, and reviewed this before each visit. As they were leaving his office, large smiles as always, Helen said: "We have a Wednesday night canasta game at the clubhouse. They're always in need of one more player. Would you be interested?"

"I used to play years ago when my wife was alive. I don't remember the rules all that well."

"It's a whole new game these days. It's called Modern American Canasta, nothing like your grandmother's rules. We have another friend who wants to learn. We could teach you both. Julia is very nice and not at all competitive."

"Is this a set-up?" Doc said with an embarrassed laugh." You know I'm seventy-six and one perfect marriage is enough for this lifetime."

"She's just a good friend who needs a canasta partner. No expectations, no agenda."

"OK, I'm game. I'll give it a try. Wednesday night at 6:30 sounds great."

The room filled with twenty-four players all seeming to be of retirement age. He met Julia, a slim attractive lady who had grayed with style. "I'm afraid I don't know the rules very well," she said. "Then I won't be the only one," said Doc with a smile.

Doc was greeted as a visiting dignitary, introduced all around. One man, who had become an amateur pastry chef upon retiring, had made a chocolate cheese cake and most of the rest had brought snacks, everything from cookies to pretzel nuggets. Coffee, water and lemonade were lined up on a nearby table. Doc made a mental note to bring some snacks to the next game, if they would have him back.

The Gordons had given Doc a book from the Canasta League of America, which he had studied like a medical text. He relaxed as he realized he knew enough not to slow down the game. At break time between games, groups seemed to form around him when it became known he was a doctor.

Conversations began with, "I've got this strange thing going on....", or "my cousin has..." or "what do you think about..." Bill rescued him, saying: "Come on guys, this is his night off."

"It's just that we don't get a chance to chat up a doctor without the meter running," said one man. Doc answered quickly with a laugh: "Who said the meter isn't running?"

"You know a lot of us take courses at the local community college. It's for senior citizens, called OLLI, the Osher Lifelong Learning Institute. Members do the teaching. You might want to consider giving a talk or two on common medical problems. It might earn you some peace at next week's canasta game and a few more paying patients at the clinic," said Bill.

"I haven't even committed to come back next Wednesday, let alone to teach medicine after so many years."

"I hope you do come back," said Julia with such enthusiasm that the Gordon's turned to each other and smiled.

"Well, it seems I've joined a senior cult," said Doc. "So the answer is yes and maybe. Maybe as far as the lecture, and a definite "Yes" for next week's card game, if you'll have me."

"I can't wait to hear what my daughter thinks about all this," Doc mumbled to himself.

CHAPTER 10

...AND NEIGHBORS

Doc paced like an expectant father in the surgical waiting area along with Marta's husband and two adult daughters. At 7 a.m. she had passed through the swinging doors with signs in large red letters forbidding entry to unauthorized people, those who didn't rate surgical scrubs. Doc knew that half the time spent in the OR was in the pre-op area, confirming that there were no allergies, starting IVs and having a series of brief work-ups by the nurse, the hospitalist and the anesthesiologist of the day. At each step along the way Marta's name and reason for surgery would be reviewed, an "X" would be placed on the correct side of her neck where a para-thyroid gland tumor grew silently and was causing her calcium to reach worrisome levels. Even without Marta's errors in judgment and GI symptoms, the calcium level alone would have made her a surgical candidate.

It was now 10:45 a.m. and Doc's mind was wandering to the dark places that house the fear of unknown complications. Just as he was about to pick up the intercom and ask for an update, the swinging doors opened and the surgeon led with "She's fine," words followed by sighs of relief and "Gracias a Dios."

"The surgery went well. The tumor came out easily and looks benign. We'll have to keep her for a while and make sure her calcium level doesn't bottom out. You can see her in the post-op area in about half an hour." Doc thanked his old friend and was once again reassured that the initial pathology was benign. Doc spoke to Jose, Marta's husband and reaffirmed the message of reassurance.

"Please give Marta my best wishes and tell her I'll be back tomorrow," said Doc. "I'll leave you all to visit, and don't be upset if she's a little groggy. It's normal after general anesthesia."

When Doc arrived home he was surprised to see someone sitting under his carport, then shocked when he realized who it was...Mrs. Greenberg, whose crone-like presence was never a welcome event. She can't be blaming Marta for turfing her lawn again. Doc girded for confrontation.

"Oh there you are, thank God," she said. Of all the possible greetings, this one surprised Doc to the point of being speechless. He waited.

"It's Ira, my husband. He won't go. I called Fire Rescue yesterday, and they said there were no signs of an emergency, so they couldn't take him to the hospital. Ira won't pay the hundreds of dollars if we call an ambulance ourselves."

"Let's back up a little. What made you call Rescue?"

"I couldn't get him in the car by myself, I've got a bad back."

"No, no. I mean what was wrong with your husband that upset you?"

"You know that Ira has always been overweight. And he had that gastric bypass three years ago. He lost over a hundred pounds, but now he's been cheating. I found bottles of Coca Cola in the garage. He admitted that he was sipping on a large bottle all day long. He said the sugar gave him energy. It also made him regain most of his weight. He's back at three hundred-fifty now, and he can't walk, says his legs hurt and won't carry him more than a few steps. He puffs like a steam engine just going from his wheelchair to the bathroom. I think those Fire Rescue guys saw an overweight guy and blamed him, like it was a character flaw or something. He's tried to be good. It's hard when there are so many things he would like to do that he can't." She began to cry.

"Let's go see him," said Doc, as he took his medical bag from the trunk of his Camry.

"Don't be shocked. He's blown up."

Doc wasn't shocked, nor was he pleased by Ira's appearance. He was in a wheelchair; the legs of his sweatpants had been slit to make room for the red tree trunks protruding. Doc could see the blistering from the doorway. Ira said: "Thanks for... coming over... Doc. I know... you and my...wife haven't been on the best... of terms."

"Don't worry about that Ira, water over the dam. Is it hard to breathe?"

"No more than..I expect ..with this big gut."

"Let's make it easier. I'll ask a question and you can just say yes or no, or nod if you wish." Ira lifted his right hand off the wheelchair arm and made a weak thumbs up sign.

"Does your chest hurt?" Head shakes side to side.

"Is your breathing getting worse?" Head shakes yes. "If the Rescue guys... saw me today... I'd be in the hospital."

"Have your legs been that swollen for a long time?"

"Couple of weeks."

"Any racing of your heart?" His head nods.

"But not when Rescue was here," said Mrs. Greenberg. "They did an EKG and said it was OK. But he's much worse today. I feel stupid calling them out again, unless you think it's necessary."

Doc unbuttoned Ira's shirt and noticed the neck veins full and with subtle pulsations. There were decreased breath sounds at the bottom of both lungs. Doc tapped on Ira's back from the top where the sound was like a drum, to the bottom where it was like the flat sound of pounding on a full container of milk. The right side of his anterior chest rose just a bit with each heartbeat and there was a soft murmur, also on the right. Doc pressed on Ira's legs and left a deep imprint. They were tender below the knees. He felt the calf muscles and then repeated the maneuver when he thought there was a rope-like density that resisted compression. The second gentle squeeze confirmed his concerns.

"Mrs. Greenberg, I want you to feel something in case I'm not here when the Fire Rescue crew arrives. Do you feel that ropey density in Ira's right calf?" He guided her fingers over the area and she shook her head yes.

"That is most likely a blood clot in a vein. The problem is that these clots often break off, go through the circulation and lodge in the lungs."

"So I was right. You see Ira. We really need to get to the hospital. And if they want to charge for an ambulance, I'll give them a piece of my mind."

"Do you understand what I just said, Ira?" said Doc. "This can be treated, but if not it is quite a dangerous situation. The clots are most probably the reason you are so short of breath. The weight doesn't help and we'll have to address that once the blood clots have been treated."

"It's just there's..nothing to do.. all day."

"OK, save your breath. There is always a cardiac rehab program later, along with some dietary advice. But that's down the road. For now let's get the ball rolling," Doc dialed rescue, identified himself as a physician and the words "pulmonary emboli" became attached to Ira's file.

⚊⧓⧓⚊

Two weeks later:

"So Ira, how are you feeling?"

"So much better. Thanks to you and Dr. Stewart. He told me you were old colleagues and he treated me like family. The invasive radiologists dissolved the biggest clot in my lungs and I feel like I can breathe again. They gave me water pills and a couple of shots and I've lost ten pounds. You can see it in my legs." Doc agreed.

"So Mrs. Greenberg, quite an adventure."

"Please call me Dotty. And how is your housekeeper doing? I heard from my girl that she's having surgery."

"Marta is doing well and should be back to work soon."

"Then neither of you should be turfing my lawn in the near future," she said with a wink.

Doc just grinned.

CHAPTER 11
MARCEY'S STORY

8 years ago

It was a busy Saturday lunch crowd, when Marcey felt the mood change before hearing it. She was in the back making four orders of toast when the murmur increased and the sound of scraping chairs could be heard. Several tables of diners were standing around an elderly lady who was slumped forward on her table. Marcey dropped the toast and pushed through the crowd. She knew Mrs. Charles, a regular who had just returned after being hospitalized for a stroke. Her walker was folded in the back of the restaurant with the booster seats. Several people were on their cell phones calling 911.

Marcey shook the immobile woman and asked her companions:

"What happened?"

At that time she was the best waitress at *The Corner Deli*. Marcey seemed to know what people wanted before they ordered, would chat up customers and loved to entertain their small children. She taught them how to make mountains from coffee creamers, or spindly spiders made of twisted straw covers which came alive when a drop of water was placed on them. There was always something to keep the little ones occupied.

Years ago, when she had completed one year of college, the lime packing plant closed in favor of cheaper imported fruit from Central America, and her Dad joined the unemployment line. He insisted she continue at the local Junior college, but she would have none of it. Half of her tips went toward the rent and grocery bills. She saved most of the rest.

A friend from college was enrolled in a nursing program leading to an RN degree and she strongly suggested that Marcey join her. She could work weekends at the restaurant and attend classes during the week. "It's a great profession and a ticket to financial security."

"But I'll be thirty when I finish."

"You'll be thirty anyway, so you might as well be doing something you love." There was one obstacle, algebra. It was a pre-requisite and Marcey thought she was no math whiz. Joan, a loyal customer and a retired science teacher, overheard and did what teachers do. Her kitchen table soon overflowed with 'Algebra for Dummies', basic geometry texts and 'Algebra for Real Dummies.' She relearned the equations and eventually said, "Marcey, come over for lunch and let me serve you for once. I'll prove that I do indeed have a kitchen and we'll serve Algebra for dessert. I promise if you ingest a little at a time, it won't cause choking."

The first lesson was to be an hour, but lasted four. Each time a chapter was finished, Marcey wanted to start the next. When a seemingly unsolvable equation was encountered, they puzzled it out together or texted it to Joan's son-in-law, an engineer. In three such sessions, each shorter than the one before, the brick wall of 'I can't' came down one correct answer at a time.

Marcey's pre-nursing courses fell before her shotgun intellect like so many clay discs tossed in the air. With each course came straight A's and increased confidence. She was accepted into a full time RN program, paid for by the local hospital in exchange for a promise to work there one year for each year of funded education. She could still earn tips on weekends, the busiest time at the restaurant.

Her clinical rotations made all that came before seem less like drudgery and more like prelude. She loved most her elective with a nurse mid-wife where she actually brought life into this world. Pediatric nursing was her second favorite rotation. The kids were so much more than small adults. They had less guile, laughed more easily and carried little of the baggage that weighed down adults.

Marcey received her RN degree with honors and was immediately offered a position on the OB floor. For two years she diagnosed labor, comforted her patients and eventually began to teach medical students the basics of delivering a baby. More than once it was suggested that she ought to consider medical school. She was a natural with patients and her struggles with math had proven that she could master anything. She eventually transferred to pediatrics for two more years before the chief nurse on her floor urged Marcey to consider entering a nurse practitioner program. She had already taken enough nursing education credits to earn a Bachelor of Science in nursing.

"It's two more years of study, which the hospital will pay for. At the end of the program, you'll pass a licensing exam—I have no doubt you will pass—and then you can practice on your own or under the direct supervision of a doctor." Her dad had long since found work in a Home Depot gardening section and no longer needed her financial support. She could save even more towards a house where she and Brent, a lab supervisor at the hospital, could start their lives together.

It was strange functioning as a doctor but not being called one. The title, nurse didn't fit either. She settled for Marcey. In the hospital the role of nurse practitioner was never clearly defined. More than once she had been handed a bedpan or been asked by a harried doctor to

"Clean up this mess." She refused to be insulted and did what she could to help out. In moments of insecurity she thought back to her first 'patient'.

⚔

"What happened?"

"The lady was eating then she stopped talking, flailed her arms and collapsed. Marcey had seen a TV show about Dr. Heimlich and his maneuver but had never tried one. She stood behind Mrs. Charles, reached around her and pulled in a sudden upward motion resulting in several audible 'pops'. A lump of corned beef shot across the table and a loud musical intake of breath followed. Soon thereafter she cried out in pain and put her hands over her lower chest. Unfortunately, Marcey had placed her arms over the patient's lower ribs whose cartilage cracked with the Heimlich compression. By the time Fire Rescue arrived, the patient was awake and complaining loudly about chest pain.

"I've never done it before," said Marcey. "I didn't mean to hurt her." The Captain of the rescue squad had seen it all and believed in unvarnished truth.

"This woman was dead. Now she's alive. You saved her life, 100 %, guaranteed. The cartilage fractures will set in two weeks and heal completely in six. You've got nothing to apologize for."

Though clinics were being started in every pharmacy, most manned by nurse practitioners, Marcey preferred independence. She also liked the day shift so she and Brent could actually spend time together. They had seen too many medical marriages end because couples saw each other only at shift change. That would not be their fate especially since they hoped to have children.

After Marcey's two years of Nurse Practitioner training she graduated to the Free Clinic, which had been one of her favorite rotations as a trainee. Shortly after her arrival, the clinic doctor moved to North Carolina and Marcey was truly on her own. Doc was a God-send. Marcey was the utility infielder of the clinic; she could care for all comers: pregnant women, new babies, general pediatrics and even adult medical patients.

She may not know everything, but she sure could do a Heimlich.

CHAPTER 12

AN ACCIDENTAL ENCOUNTER

It was Marcey's birthday and Doc was determined to make it special. After the last morning patients, they drove together to a local Greek restaurant that Marcey had praised. Her favorite chocolate layer cake was in a cooler on the back seat, hidden beneath Doc's raincoat, They were about to cross the highway when a motorcycle raced a red light on US1 and lost, cutting in front of them. Doc crushed the brake and narrowly avoided the Kawasaki. The driver in the left turn lane was not so lucky, impaling the motorcycle on his front bumper, the car emitting the sickening wail of brakes, crunching metal followed by the dull thud of a body tossed against unforgiving asphalt.

Traffic in all four directions froze as doors flung open and people rushed to help. The first was Marcey with a surprisingly spry Doc two steps behind. Marcey was the lead blocker plowing her way through onlookers with Doc in her wake.

The motorcyclist, still in his air force flight jacket, was lying with his neck flexed unnaturally.

"Can you hear me? What's your name?" asked Doc, as he caught his breath.

"I can't move… Pete… I can't move." Doc noted that the motorcyclist was slim and muscular but had to take a breath between every few words.

"I'm a doctor and Marcey's a nurse practitioner and we'll take care of you Pete."

"Marcey can you get the emergency kit from my car? Can someone go into that grocery store and get two one-pound bags of sugar or flour," he shouted. Doc gently straightened Pete's head and held it in place with two hands. When the two bags of sugar arrived he placed them so they immobilized the victim's neck. One onlooker was given the task of making sure the neck didn't move even a millimeter.

"Squeeze my fingers," said Doc placing them in Pete's palm. Nothing. He tried again on the other side, Nothing. There was no movement of the legs no matter how hard Doc urged or how scrunched up were Pete's eyebrows trying to wish life back into his limbs.

"God no… I'm a quad… never fly again," he gasped.

"We don't know that," said Doc, just as Marcey arrived with the emergency kit.

Doc noted that the patient was not moving much air and asked for and got a safety pin. He touched the point to Pete's skin starting at the waist and moving upward. There was no feeling below the C-4 dermatome, the area of skin controlled by the nerve from his neck, the same nerve that made the diaphragm contract. A medical school pneumonic rang in Doc's head: *C-3, 4, 5 keeps the diaphragm alive.* There was not much innervation left to keep Pete breathing.

Doc pulled Marcey aside. His jaw was clenched and there was sweat on his brow. "I think his neck injury is high enough that he's not ventilating. He'll have to be intubated. I haven't passed an endotracheal tube in a really long time."

"No problem Doc," said Marcey, still panting from the run to her car. We had to take an OB anesthesia rotation. If I could intubate patients thrashing around in labor I should be able to do this."

"Pete, we're going to have to put in a tube to help you breathe," said Doc.

"Let me die."

"Lots of people get better after the initial nerve trauma and swelling recedes."

"Let me die... No wheel chair."

"We don't know what the outcome will be, but people can walk away from injuries like these."

"Bullshit ... Never fly."

"But you'll have a shot at living, having a family. Are you one to run from a challenge, to let something beat you without a fight? Look, if you want to give up you'll have lots of opportunities. But you only get one chance to decide if you'll be here tomorrow. We need to numb up your throat and put a breathing tube in."

"And... tomorrow?"

"Then that's your choice. Not one I agree with, but it's your choice."

"OK... do it... Won't quit...yet."

Marcey sedated him with some IV versed, numbed his throat with cetacaine spray so foul tasting that it made him wince, and placed the tube on the first pass. She taped it into place as Doc attached the Ambu Bag and compressed it, filling Pete's lungs and causing his chest to rise and his skin to lose its bluish discoloration.

Fire rescue arrived, immobilized Pete's neck with a brace and rolled him onto a board. The rescue Captain motioned Doc and Marcey to the side. It took Doc a long moment for his knees to decide to support his body after fifteen minutes of kneeling.

"What were you thinking?" fumed the Captain. "This kid will be a quad. You should have let him die."

Doc's first choice of words was laced with profanity, but then he said: "It's easy to judge in retrospect, isn't it Captain? This boy, this twenty year old boy has a totally intact brain. We talked and *he decided* to be intubated. We're medical people not executioners."

"I've seen what happens to these kids as their spirit and body shrivel up. It happened to my cousin. It was death by a thousand medical procedures."

"I've seen far too many patients with high cervical spine injuries as you have described," replied Doc. "But I had a couple of patients that I followed for decades after their necks were stabilized, the spinal shock abated and their limbs began to work again. Our job is to give this young man a chance to live. He'll have lots of other chances to quit."

"OK, maybe you have a point. We'll see. But I wouldn't have done what you did."

The patient was then loaded gently into the rescue ambulance for the short drive to the helicopter landing site, then airlifted to the trauma center.

"You really saved the day Marcey," said Doc.

"I'm still not sure we did the right thing but thanks," she said.

"One of the things I learned in my medical school training was the natural history of disease. I learned that there are lots of situations, like metastatic cancer, where the outcome for most is predetermined the day we see them. But some people defy the odds and are alive years later. Our job is not to save everyone, just to give them a chance, to give them hope."

"Well maybe this young man will be one of the lucky ones. I'll check in on him tomorrow on my way to the clinic," she said.

"By the way, that was a very slick intubatrion. What other tricks did they teach you in NP training?"

"If you ever need an emergency C-section just give me a ring, but right now let's share a piece of my birthday cake you've been hiding in the back seat."

CHAPTER 13
ASLEEP AT THE WHEEL

Doc looked forward to the weekly canasta game. He was comfortable with the basics and was now trying to master some of the strategy. Julia too was learning and they worked well as partners. Bill and Helen, their opponents, seemed preoccupied tonight. Helen didn't remove her gaze from Bill's face. Bill didn't seem to be concentrating on the game. When the first break came, Doc asked Bill,

"Are you guys OK? You seem concerned about something other than who can meld."

"I nearly drove off the road coming here. I guess I lost focus. Helen says I fell asleep and she had to grab the wheel. She's been going on and on about my not driving. Well let me tell you: This cowboy is not giving up his pony, nor do I plan to become an Uber addict. Everyone loses concentration once in a while. We didn't hit anything."

"Are you getting enough sleep?"

"Lots of hours in bed. I wake up frequently and disturb Helen, so she goes to the second bedroom."

"Do you snore?"

"She says I do, but I'm not aware of it. I am tired all the time. I do tend to miss more of conversations than I used to. Maybe my hearing is going too."

"Do you mind if I act more like your doctor and less like your friend? I'd like to ask the eye witness, what she saw."

"I guess, but don't be surprised if she blows this all out of proportion. She was a lot more shook up than I was."

Doc met Helen at the snack table. She wasn't talking to anyone. She and her cookie were in another time and place. "Hi Helen." She didn't answer immediately and Doc tried again. "Bill told me what happened. That must have been terrifying."

"I thought we were going to die. His head was on his chest and we were headed right for a tree. I screamed and turned the wheel away. He woke up and hit the brake. That's never happened before. He would nod off watching TV but lately it's worse. He fell asleep Saturday night while we were talking to the Wilsons in our living room. My uncle behaved like that and he wound up having a brain tumor. If Bill does..." her face was desolation itself.

"Does he take anything to help him sleep, pills, perhaps a drink or two at night?"

"He does like a nightcap to help him relax."

"How about his weight? Any change recently?"

"He has gotten into the habit of ice cream after dinner, and he's gone up at least one belt size."

"Now the million dollar question. Does he snore?"

"Like a bull in heat." Doc smiled. He hadn't heard that description before.

"How about you both come see me at the clinic tomorrow, and you drive."

"I'll hide his keys if I have to."

At the clinic Bill was still grumbling about not driving his own car. Doc took a detailed history then examined the patient's throat... narrow, no large tonsils but a big uvula hanging down in the middle. Doc then measured Bill's neck at 18 inches.

"I'm not buying shirts here Doc."

"There's a magic number, 18 inches, which is associated with a very high incidence of sleep disordered breathing. You probably know it as sleep apnea. You also have a small opening in your throat which I suspect has gotten smaller as you gained weight."

"How does putting a few pounds on my waistline make me fall asleep at the wheel? That's a stretch don't you think."

"Actually it makes perfect sense," said Doc. "Your throat muscles relax in sleep partly obstructing your airway causing a snore. Increased weight makes the airway even narrower. Every time you get into deep sleep the airway can close completely and no air passes. Your oxygen level drops and you awaken, sometimes more than once every minute."

"But I'm not aware of waking up."

"Most people aren't. Your brain doesn't get the rest it needs, and it tries to make up for it with micro-sleeps, literally short periods of sleep while you think you're awake."

"So that's how I can drive off the road and remember none of it."

"Bingo," said Doc.

"So?"

"So we get you to spend one night in a sleep lab. They'll hook you up to more equipment than you thought possible, but you will sleep. If they prove sleep apnea they'll start positive pressure using a mask over your nose and adjust the pressure to keep your airway open. You may even get your wife back in the bedroom, since your snoring will decrease or vanish completely. Once you're more awake, the car keys come back too."

"What about sleeping pills or my nightcap."

"Neither will be necessary and both will make the problem worse."

"You know I can still beat you at canasta, half asleep."

"Not for long," said Doc.

⚒

That night as they were finishing their dreaded computer entries, Doc challenged Marcey to a game he had played as an intern.

"OK Marcey, time for a game called *What's My Diagnosis.*"

"How does it work?"

"We ask each other a question related to a patient we've seen and keep score of how many we can answer. I'll go first, if that's OK."

"Sure, it will give me time to think of my question."

"You know Marcey, I told you about Bill and Helen. His sleep problem reminded me of another patient. I saw a minister last week, the gentlest soul ever, who punched his wife while both were sleeping. He was mortified, she was hurt and angry. He never had any violent tendencies before. The minister said he was dreaming that a burglar had broken into their bedroom and he was defending the family."

"I know that one Doc. We studied about REM Behavior disorder where the usual muscle paralysis we all have during dreams, disappears. One point for the Nurse Practitioner."

"I had one patient years ago who was dreaming he was in a football game," Doc added. He tackled his dresser and broke his collar bone. Thank goodness it's easily treated with Klonopin."

"I've got one," said Marcey. "You know the old saying that strange diagnoses occur in threes. I think I saw number three in our series this morning. A Mom was convinced her eight year old was hyperactive, inattentive at school, jumping around. He never slept through the night and kept getting sore throats."

"What did you find on physical?"

"Oh, we're allowed to ask questions?"

"Yes but they have to be specific to this patient."

"Any more rules I should know?"

"I'll let you know when I make them up," said Doc.

"I looked in his mouth and saw his tonsils kissing in the midline."

"Does he snore?"

"Mom said he snores enough to wake the other children."

"I don't see many kids but I have heard that kids with sleep apnea due to upper airway obstruction often don't complain of sleepiness but present like Attention-Deficit Hyperactivity Dosorder. Thankfully it's cured with a tonsillectomy."

"So, is there some official score sheet?" said Marcey.

"Well this computer must be good for something," said Doc.

CHAPTER 14

CHARITY BEGINS AT HOME

Doc and Marcey drove back to the clinic after lunch past the gauntlet of people holding signs, all ending with 'God Bless You'. Some began with 'Homeless Please Help'. One used the word 'Veteran', carried by a man in camo pants and jacket. Some went right to the core, 'Hungry Please Help'. Others asked for work. There were more women than Doc remembered seeing.

"What do you do about them Marcey?"

"I don't give cash because I don't want it going for drugs or alcohol. I used to hand out a card with the names and addresses of shelters and places that feed the homeless. I found that most were discarded before the next car was approached. I feel stingy if I don't give and conned if I do."

"So you keep the windows rolled up and look away feeling guilty, like I do," said Doc. "I knew a clergyman who always gave a dollar. He explained that if the money was used in a bar it was not his sin, but not giving at all would be. I'm not comfortable treating a condition and not knowing if the treatment is doing any good," Doc continued.

"Well we do see patients in our clinic who come from the shelter, and even give them meds for free. We do what we can," said Marcey.

Doc still believed he was rationalizing, nibbling around the edges and not getting to the heart of the problem. What are the symptoms that all these people have in common? The word 'hungry' populated each sign. Was the answer so simple? thought Doc.

His next clinic day he arose a bit earlier than usual and went to the kitchen. Trying not to make too much noise, he laid out his instruments needed for this operation. The plastic bags, the peanut butter, the jelly, the bread. He melded the ingredients in the 2:1 ratio he remembered loving as a kid –twice as much peanut butter, sweetened with just enough jelly, not so much that it was a jelly doughnut dripping purple with the first bite. He loaded seven sandwiches, that was all the bread he had, into his Styrofoam cooler on top of two ice packs and a layer of water bottles.

It was getting to the punishing heat and humidity of summer in South Florida. Thankfully Doc's senior citizen of a Camry still had air conditioning. Doc brought the cooler into the clinic since he knew the car's temperature would soar over 100 degrees when left in the parking lot.

At lunch time he drove to the local Subway sandwich shop. Those asking for help were out in the mid-day heat. This time Doc rolled down his window and instead of cash offered a sandwich, a drink and a handshake. Most were happy to receive these and Doc noted the sandwiches were not discarded, at least not immediately. One lady questioned the contents, saying, "I'm a vegetarian. No meat in this is there?" Doc reassured her, was careful to tell everyone about peanut allergy, and none refused the food. The one problem was that Doc ran out quickly. By the time one mid-forties man came by, Doc had to apologize and say he'd see him tomorrow with more sandwiches. The Veteran said, "No problem Captain, I'll see you then," and smiled a broad yellow toothed grin, which was the warmest reaction Doc had elicited.

Though he was not scheduled to work that Thursday, he made sure to buy more bread, and Costco-sized containers of grape jelly and peanut butter. He made a dozen sandwiches and bought a second cooler for water. At lunch time on this particularly asphalt melting day, he retraced his usual route. He recognized many of the sign carriers.

Finally he saw the man who had been promised a sandwich. He was weaving and looked to be intoxicated. A deputy sheriff was approaching him but the man seemed not to understand the conversation. Doc pulled his car to the curb and parked. As he approached the Veteran, the officer said, "Do you know this man, old timer?" "We've met before. I'm a doctor from the free clinic. Might I just take a minute to talk to him?"

"OK if you can get him out of the street."

Doc said, "I brought you that sandwich like I promised yesterday. Come with me to the shade and you can eat it." The man dragged his sign as he let Doc lead him to a bench. Doc noted the redness of the man's face and the fact that he was not sweating. Almost everyone on the street had droplets of sweat from upper lip to brow. Doc could feel the heat radiating off the man.

"Officer, would it be possible to bring this man to our clinic. It's only around the block. The hospital is at least twenty minutes away."

"If he'll cooperate."

"I'll go with him in the back seat of your patrol car to be sure he does, if that's OK."

"It's OK with me if you don't think he's violent."

"I haven't seen anything to suggest that. Getting off the street into AC may go a long way to making him better." And so Doc found himself on his day off being delivered to the clinic in the back seat of a Broward sheriff's car along with a patient. The deputy steadied his charge, while keeping a wary eye on him.

Doc found out the patient's name, Rick Franklin, from his old military ID, no known address. Other formalities were delayed as a thermometer was placed in Rick's mouth. Marcey had a look of concern as she showed Doc the thermometer, 106 degrees. They repeated the measurement and got the same answer. His heart rate was 130 and blood pressure 110/90. As Marcey started an IV, Doc made ice packs and placed them in Rick's armpits. They lowered his camo pants and placed two more cold packs in the area of his femoral arteries.

They called for an ambulance.

Doc asked, "Rick, has this ever happened to you before?"

"Once, they had to put me in an ice bath. That was awful, shivering to beat all hell."

"Are you taking any drugs, cocaine, PCP?"

"No. Some weed, that's all."

"Any allergy or psychiatric medicines?"

"Just Benadryl. It helps me sleep."

"How long have you been taking it?"

"I just started." By now half of the IV bottle had been absorbed. They rechecked his temperature and it was 104. Some of Rick's facial flush began to fade making him look like the man Doc had seen yesterday.

"Where is that ambulance?" asked Marcey.

The deputy answered, "There is a multicar accident on the Turnpike, sometimes all the sirens in the world won't open up the road. At least he's getting some treatment here."

"Rick, you will still have to go to the hospital to make sure your fever hasn't caused muscle damage which can injure your kidneys. And you've got to stay away from Benadryl and any other allergy medicines. They prevent sweating so your body can overheat like this again."

They could see Ricks mind clearing as the IV's went in and as his temperature fell.

"Hey Doc. Don't think you can get off that easy."

"What do you mean?"

"You still owe me that sandwich."

CHAPTER 15
SECRETS

Doc did a double take when he saw Robert and Barbara Whiteside in his waiting room. He had seen them every Wednesday evening at canasta for months. He, an accountant and she, his office manager hadn't missed a session. Doc didn't know them well, but was aware they drove a Tesla sedan of the $90,000 price range rarely seen in the Free Clinic parking lot.

"Is it Wednesday night or am I hallucinating?"

"Neither, we just wanted to get Robert's blood pressure checked. It's been a while and our family doctor's office is chaos itself. His new associates are so young, like the policemen these days. They look like they're just out of high school. It seems we're turning our lives over to children."

"All evidence to the contrary," said Doc smiling. "I last saw New Utrecht High School over sixty years ago."

"We've come to know and trust you," said Barbara.

"Have a seat and let's talk," said Doc.

"How long have you had high blood pressure, Robert?"

"He's had it for fifteen years, since Robbie our first grandchild was born. Guess he was really excited about that."

"As he should be. Any heart attack, angina or stroke?"

"No, he's avoided those."

"How about any other serious illnesses...Robert?" said Doc as he looked his patient in the eye.

The question was met with a big smile and silence.

"Barbara interjected: "We really do have to go. We have an appointment in thirty minutes. Maybe we could get a prescription for his blood pressure medicine and continue this at another time. It is tax season, which is crazy busy for us."

Doc gave them a prescription for a thirty day supply of medication, and elicited a promise that they would return for a real visit after the April rush. Then, with the acceleration of a Tesla, they were gone. Doc wondered: "What just happened?" The missing pieces far outnumbered those he had been permitted to see.

The Whitesides were no shows at canasta that week and the next and the next. Doc asked his friends, but Bill and Helen only guessed that the cause was internment by tax season, and liberation day would be April 16th.

The second visit to the clinic was early in May. "The thirty day supply goes quickly," said Barbara.

"Well I hope you have a little more time to talk."

"Sure," said Robert.

Doc tapped the computer screen and said: "My accessory brain tells me we never got to past medical history." Have you had any operations Robert?"

"What I'd really like to talk about is my bowels. I'm constipated all the time. I try prunes and fiber but all I get is gas."

"He had his tonsils out as a kid and had disc surgery in his lower back in 2008, just in time for the financial crash. What a zoo that was," said Barbara.

"The recuperation period from disc surgery can be long. How did you meet with your clients Robert?"

"Oh I did that," said Barbara, "I've been doing that for years."

"Are you an accountant also?"

"No, I'm the office manager. Speaking of which, I really do need to get back. We're taking up way too much of your time. We just need a ninety day supply of meds with a few refills."

"Oh I've got time, and tax season is over, so no reason to rush off."

"What about my bowels?"

"We'll get to that Robert. Have you had a colonoscopy?"

"No he hasn't."

Doc looked straight at Barbara and said, "I notice that you tend to answer for Robert."

"Not really, well I guess I do. That's what happens when you've been married forty-two years."

"Mind if I ask your husband a few questions?"

Barbara shifted in her chair, "Well if it's quick."

"Robert, I'm going to give you three words. I want you to remember them—Blue, Shoelace and Uncle." The patient repeated them.

"Now do you get abdominal pain when you are constipated?"

"Sometime."

"How bad, from one to ten."

"Oh, about a two."

"What were the three words Robert?"

"What three words?"

Barbara looked down at her pocket book; her head slumped so Doc couldn't see her face.

"How long Barbara?" asked Doc.

"I first noticed the memory loss after his back surgery. Back then he occasionally got a date wrong. He never did that before. Then over the years the memory gaps grew and he began making up answers to fill in. For the last five years I took over the business. I can file tax forms in my sleep. It's all computerized now anyway."

"But you're not an accountant."

"The clients don't notice the difference; never once did they question my work. How else can I keep the practice going?"

"It might be time to think about selling it and relieving your burden. Then maybe you won't be afraid to get Robert evaluated properly. This could be Alzheimer's but it could also be a series of mini-strokes. We might be able to prevent the next one."

"I won't be happy to lose the income, but I must admit I feel relieved, like it's the end of tax season."

"Hiding things takes so much energy. Sometimes it's draining," said Doc. Barbara began to cry softly as Doc handed her a tissue.

Doc gave her the name of a dementia specialist at the University Hospital. He included the phone number of a local caregiver support group.

"Now Robert, let's get that colonoscopy scheduled."

CHAPTER 16
FIRST DO NO HARM

Doc felt as if he were watching an imminent train wreck and was helpless to stop it. Alice, a smile on her frequently enhanced lips, left with the medical clearance she came for.

"I've always wanted the flat stomach of European supermodels. This tummy tuck will do that. And Doc, doesn't my nose look so much better without that awful bump? And my chin," she said, rotating her head side to side so he wouldn't be deprived of the unforgettable vista. The only thing awful about her nose to Doc was the fact that she paid thousands of her hard earned dollars to smooth out a bump visible only to her and her plastic surgeon.

"You look fine, Alice. I'm glad you're happy with the result. May I ask about these operations? This is the fifth, if I'm not mistaken."

"You forgot my boob job when I was sixteen."

"You are a very attractive woman. What is the point of all this surgery?"

"Well in the modern parlance Doc, 'Duh'. To be beautiful of course."

"It must be costing you a fortune. You told me your plastic surgeon drives a Bentley. Someone's paying for that, and I bet you've bought more than one bumper yourself."

"It's all a matter of priorities Doc. Looking better makes me happy, so I save my money and when I have enough, I fix one piece of the puzzle."

"Did you always feel this way, that you needed to improve your looks?"

"My sister was always the good looking one, the glamorous one. She got the modeling job right after high school. I was the good girl, the latch key kid who made dinner for everyone, shopped and cleaned the house—a very imperfect Cinderella."

"Didn't you tell me that you are the district's Special Ed. advisor? And that after school you tutor for hours?"

"Where do you think I get the beautification bucks?" she said with a laugh. "And don't worry Doc, they've already had me seen by the psychiatrist—narcissistic maybe, but crazy, no."

Doc didn't bother asking why she came to his lower cost clinic for a medical clearance before surgery.

Savings has to start somewhere.

As big as the smile on Alice's face, was the frown on Mrs. Davis when they passed in the hall. She was exuding complaints, like some offensive perfume, even before getting into the exam room. "Good morning Mrs. Davis"—the form of address she preferred.

"My back hurts every time I bend and I can't digest fatty foods. Could I have pancreatic cancer?"

"I learned in medical school that the answer to any question beginning with the word *could*, is always yes, even if it is a one in a million chance. But the question should be: Is it likely enough to spend time and money to investigate the symptom?"

"But why am I having the pain?"

"I can't answer why for many symptoms. Did you know that normal people, even those a lot younger than you, have symptoms at any given time: pains, aches, constipation, burping? If we investigated each one, you'd spend your entire day getting tests."

"But what if we miss something? My aunt had belly pain that they told her was irritable bowel, till they finally opened her up and closed her—cancer," she whispered.

"There is the concept of risk vs. benefit. There is a risk of pursuing symptoms."

"How so?"

"I saw a 28 year old young woman patient shortly before I retired. She came in complaining of vague lower abdominal discomfort. We did blood tests, upper and lower endoscopies, CT scans....all negative other than a few small fibroids. Even blood markers for ovarian and pancreatic cancer...nada. I recommended waiting and watching and treating symptomatically.

She kept doctor shopping and finally found one whom she talked into doing exploratory surgery, an extensive procedure, which showed no disease. She got a wound infection and developed blood clots in her legs that spread to her lungs. She nearly died, of too much testing, unnecessary medical care."

"Well that's all well and good, but I don't want to be one of those people that you guys pat on the head and say everything's fine, right up to the time I keel over. If you won't do more, I'll see someone at the University who will."

"Let me give you the phone number of a good gastroenterologist who will give you an honest opinion. And if he agrees that we should follow you closely but do nothing else, then please believe him."

⚔ ⚔

6 p.m.

"Marcey, there are days I might as well have stayed home," said Doc. "Some people just don't seem to understand that you don't have to be sick to have symptoms."

"You are preaching to the choir Doc. At the end of a busy clinic day, I can't wait to go home and soak in a hot tub. My symptoms dissolve in that wonderful steamy water."

"It's not something they discuss in school, but normal people do get symptoms frequently. I remember reading the results of a phone survey where the average healthy person had five or more symptoms in a single week, things like fatigue or headache."

"So our challenge is finding out which of those five has a harmful cause," said Marcey.

"That's the art of medicine. I'm sure that the need for reassurance accounts for half the tests done in this country."

"Fear of malpractice suits accounts for many, also." said Marcey.

"Most folks can put up with symptoms if they are not disabling. Then there are those like Mrs. Davis. It would be so much easier on everyone if the patient accepts the results of reasonable amounts of testing," said Doc.

"What a tightrope we have to walk," said Marcey.

"Well I always remember what they taught me in the first week of medical school.

Primum Non Nocere...First do no harm."

"Words to live by," said Marcey.

CHAPTER 17
DOC'S STORY

As a young boy, Doc's family rented the first floor of a private home in Brooklyn, NY, and he never wanted for anything. Of course those things missing were labeled luxury, and as such, unnecessary or ostentatious. The important things were the roof overhead, Mom's lamb stew on Friday night and 52nd street where a dozen heads would emerge from closed doors at the first sound of a bouncing ball. And there was PS 180, which housed his favorite teacher, a burly army veteran who introduced Doc to poetry as well as the three R's. To this day he could still recite 'The Highwayman' and a few verses of 'Richard Corey'. He wondered what it said that both poems ended in violence. Doc was not a violent person. Having older siblings he inherited the parental concessions extracted by his sibs with wolverine-like tenacity. He was the compromiser, the one who placated, who got more with honey than vinegar. The city schools provided a high quality product at an irresistible price of zero dollars, including four years at Brooklyn College. He went to The Medical College of Virginia, 300 miles away in distance but culturally removed by light years. He learned that the direct speech of New York City, shorn of any subtlety, could be replaced by words spoken with a gentle, non-confrontational southern drawl.

He worked. As a young teen he bottled shellac into jars and helped load trucks with five gallon metal cans of the same. In later summers he was a waiter at a cabana club. He never underestimated the commitment it took to work by the sweat of your brow, and he never under-tipped a waitperson. In med school, tuition was a combination of loans and grants. In later years he sent a generous check every year when the Foundation called, his one caveat that every penny should be used for scholarships. In medical school he was never without a job, be it the 'guard' in the Medical Education Building, or the all night lab tech in the emergency room.

He loved all aspects of medicine but loved most talking to people and helping them solve problems, for that was the essence of medicine. Each sick patient was a puzzle, a Rubik's cube that must be evaluated from all angles and gently studied to arrive at the correct conclusion. He and his med school roommate would alternate becoming the patient, their 'doctor' having to ask the right question to unlock the medical maze.

"I'm really hot all the time, and losing weight and I've got a tremor that's new. What disease do I have?" Then both would read about hyperthyroidism if they missed it, or even if they didn't. Surgery had a certain appeal. You had one thing to do and when you were scrubbed you were not to be disturbed. He found a similar unity of focus when something went wrong with medical patients at 3 a.m. No senior residents or fellows wanted to be there, and he, an intern, got to sift through the desert of distraction for the nugget of vital information. Only if overmatched did he awaken a superior. His reputation grew as a 'wall', someone who could stop most problems cold, vs. a 'sieve' who passed all problems onto more senior residents. He was prized by his program and stayed an extra year as a Chief Resident, more a staff position than one in training.

Doc developed a reputation as a caring yet aggressive physician. One night a nursing home patient was admitted with abdominal pain. He felt a mass like a large cucumber in the right upper part of her abdomen. On ultrasound the mass was shown to be a massively dilated gall bladder with a stone blocking its duct. The patient had fever and a rapid heart rate. She had many other illnesses, including a recent heart attack and emphysema that made the surgeons say the patient was not an operative candidate, that she couldn't live through surgery.

"But she'll die without surgery," said Doc, the young resident.

"I'm not going to be the executioner," said the surgeon.

Long before the time of invasive radiologists, Doc became one. He scrubbed the patient's skin with betadine, numbed the area with lidocaine and placed an intracath, a plastic tube that fits inside a needle, directly into the swollen gallbladder. All manner of foul fluid drained into a suction bottle. The patient's fever resolved, her heart rate returned to normal, then no one knew what to do with the tube. Can you pull out the tube and not spread infection? Doc was not willing to send her back to her nursing home with a tube that would undoubtedly become contaminated with antibiotic resistant organisms. None of the faculty had any wisdom to add. Doc gave more antibiotics and pulled the tube. The patient's improvement continued and she was discharged one week later. Despite his reputation, Doc knew he was not fearless, or reckless. He had analyzed the situation as well as he could and did what was best for his patient. This pretty much summed up his approach to medicine throughout his career.

He met Roberta in college, in his senior year. Her picture on his dorm room desk kept him going through the first year in medical school. He joked that the second best day of his life was the day she agreed to marry him. The first best, he said, was the day she went through with it. Of course he knew it was a lie. The best day of both their lives was the day Suzie, their only child, was born.

After training he opened his office and Roberta was his office manager, sometime front desk person and the glue that held it all together. Doc covered his own patients. If anything happened late at night he was there. He cross-covered with another physician when each desperately needed a week off. Later a third was added to the rotation. Only in Doc's last few years in practice did he not carry a beeper on weekends off. The plan was to move to a new house after he retired. Expecting lots of visitors, he and Roberta bought a three bedroom house in a retirement community, Tamarac. It was being built when Roberta's bone marrow erupted, pouring primitive leukemic cells, like lava, into the caldera of her body. Two months later she was gone and Doc was adrift for the first time in a half century.

Suzie was the first to propose a symbiotic arrangement. Doc could complete the move to Tamarac and Suzie would join him. She proposed a rent sharing agreement but he would have none of it. Just having her near would make the deal fair. She could be there for her father if something went wrong, not miles away, after all, the years were accumulating. Finally, being able to save some of her meager teacher's salary was also attractive.

They were comfortable, each respecting the other's space. Marta, their housekeeper took care of most of the hard work, and was a delight to be around. The only difficult part for Suzie, was watching her father age before her eyes, not unlike the ice sculpture at her wedding, overnight becoming a slab of slush–not unlike her brief marriage.

Suzie had to admit that these days her Dad looked more like his old self than at any time since he retired, yet she couldn't help but worry. It was his choice to work at the clinic and she'd just have to live with that. She silently pledged to keep a close eye on him and not be afraid to speak up if he flew too close to the Tamarac sun.

CHAPTER 18

ALL THAT WHISTLES

"There must be a special on pediatric asthma," said Marcey. "Half the kids with respiratory viruses are presenting with wheezing for the first time."

"It's a little strange that I've not seen that in the adults," said Doc.

"Well the day is young," she replied.

Doc heard the cough, deep as if resonating through a barrel, before he called the next patient.

"Mrs. Walsh?" She was a forty-ish lady who bore the heavily made up face of someone who wished all eyes to focus above the neck. She was probably quite attractive, thought Doc, before putting on thirty pounds with each of three pregnancies. Once she began coughing it consumed her whole being. Her body shook. She hunched forward, knees pulled up slightly and her face turned the scarlet of an overripe tomato, escaping its cosmetic disguise. The row of connected waiting room chairs rocked in unison. As the cough eventually released her, the patient managed a purposeful movement and a handkerchief materialized from one of her sleeves. She spit something into it, blew her nose, and the spasm abated taking with it her crimson color.

She walked slowly, looked back at the chair, then followed to the exam room.

"That's quite a cough. How long has this been going on?"

"This time, about a week."

"This time?"

"I keep getting the flu every couple of weeks. I started about six months ago. I had the flu shot for goodness sake."

"I'm afraid that's not how flu works," said Doc. "You can get it once and rarely twice if you're unlucky enough to get both influenza A and B, but not over and over."

"Well how else can you explain why I cough so hard I wet the furniture if I don't use Depends? It's so embarrassing. I spit up yellow stuff and sometimes it comes from my nose too."

"Do you wheeze?"

"Especially when it starts."

"Does it start suddenly or gradually?"

"So suddenly that it wakes me up in the middle of the night. I cough so hard it scares my husband. I have to sit up to breathe. The inhaler helps the wheezing after the third or fourth time I use it, but the cough goes on. I went to Urgent Care last time and they gave me a steroid, prednisone. It helped after the second or third day but it made me nuts, hyper, like I was on speed."

"Was anything going on when this started, any dust or chemical exposure, home renovation, new pet?"

"Nope, we live in the same house since we got married. It's not immaculate, but it's as clean as you can expect with three kids. Now that you mention it, the cough started when I was pretty far along with my last pregnancy."

"Any history of sinus problems or asthma in you or in your family?"

"Nope."

"How late do you eat in the evening?"

"Not you too? Are you going to blame everything on my weight, like every other doctor? I want to crawl under a table and hide every time I see my OBGYN. She gives me the fifteen minute Weight Watchers workover."

"No, I'm not going to lecture you, I promise. But I do need to know how late you eat."

"We have dinner at 6:30 every night. Then we bathe the kids and get them off to bed. After 9 we watch our programs and snack. He loves sour dough pretzels and a beer and I...."

Doc waited.

"I meet up with my two best friends, Ben and Jerry, but only one scoop, well maybe two when the carton needs finishing up. Then we go to sleep. The ice cream makes me logy and I go out like a light in minutes."

After another dozen questions and being examined, she said:

"How do I improve my immunity Doc? I don't want the kids catching this over and over."

"I don't think there is much danger of that. This doesn't seem to be a contagious disease."

"What then, why is the phlegm yellow if it's not a bacterial infection? Why does it keep coming back?"

"Whoa, lots of questions, but they all lead to one conclusion. I think what's going on here is related to your weight, but indirectly. When we sleep at night our protective reflexes relax. Liquid in our throats can go down the wrong pipe and wind up in our airway."

"But I don't eat at night."

"The liquid comes from your stomach, which is full because of the late evening snacking."

"But I've done that for years."

"Now having extra weight, especially around the middle, puts pressure on your full stomach and pushes some of that liquid into your throat and occasionally down your airway. You inhale the acid which causes a superficial burn, resulting in yellow sputum, wheezing, the whole catastrophe."

"Are you saying I'm going to need weight loss surgery?"

"There are lots of less invasive, common sense approaches that work quite well."

"I hate surgery. What can we do to avoid that?"

"I'm not crazy about it either. First we can use gravity to help us."

"I can't sleep standing up."

"No, but you can use a wedge, a triangle of foam rubber, under the head of your bed. This keeps your head above your abdomen and fluid doesn't like to run uphill."

"Seems easy enough."

"Also there is a pill we can try for a few weeks which reduces acid in the stomach. But the easiest treatment is also the hardest—to have nothing to eat or drink for three hours before bedtime."

"Oh, my poor Ben and you want me to neglect Jerry too."

"As of now they are not your friends. It means your stomach will be mostly empty when you sleep and then we've got a good shot at breaking the cycle of recurrent cough and wheezing."

"And I might lose a few pounds too. How did you do that?"

"What's that?" said Doc.

"Seems you figured out my problem and got the weight loss lecture in without my noticing it."

The next patient was one Doc had waited for weeks to see. Pat,'Don't call me Mr. Boone,' walked gingerly into the exam room. It was a month after his heart valve had been replaced. Doc noted the patient was careful to avoid the chest incision. He also noted that there was no shortness of breath or wheeze when Pat entered the exam room. Doc had gotten periodic updates on his patient. The hospital returned him to the clinic for follow up after Pat threatened to go to the administrator and the Sun Sentinel of they didn't.

"Well you damned sure cured my asthma. Haven't used an inhaler in a month. Not bad for an old guy." Doc's eyes opened wide in surprise.

"You do know that the cause of your wheezing..."

"At ease Doc. I'm just pullin' your chain. They talked a lot about cardiac asthma in the hospital. But you're the one who told 'em what's wrong. I don't care how old you are, you're gonna have to put up with my sour face for a lot more years."

The final patient that day came for a refill of nasal allergy spray. Without it every breath resulted in a whistling sound from her nose, sounding just like ...wheezing.

6 p.m.

"Hey Marcey, remember what I said about not seeing wheezing?

Never mind."

CHAPTER 19
CLOSURE

"How can they close the clinic?" said Doc.

"It's only for two or three weeks. They have to tent it; seems we have termites. Then they need to replace most of the fascia boards, whatever they are, and finally, they'll scrape off all the old paint which may or may not contain lead, and put a new coat of safer stuff on top. We sure could use a touch-up," said Marcey.

"But what are the patients going to do in the meantime?"

"The University Hospital is opening up clinic hours for our patients. They'll be seen by residents who will have access to all our charts. I knew there was some reason for having those electronic medical records we slave over every night."

"What they won't have Marcey, is you and me, providers who know the patients."

"At least they can get their meds refilled and won't miss prenatal visits."

"On the other hand, I just remembered a psychiatrist friend who went sailing all summer. He was amazed at how much better his patients were when he returned," said Doc.

"You mean we're not as vital to the health care system as we'd like to believe?"

"I learned long ago that I'm not an M-Deity, like some of my colleagues believed they were."

"Time to start packing up our samples and medical equipment, not to mention our beloved computers."

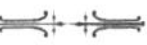

First Monday

"How come you're up so early Dad?" said Suzie.

"I couldn't sleep well, worrying about our folks and how they are going to be chewed up in that bureaucratic maw of a University Hospital."

"It wouldn't have anything to do with backsliding to the ranks of the unemployed?"

"I guess the boredom, or anticipation of it, is weighing on my mind."

"What are you going to do all day?"

"You'll think this is compulsive to the extreme, but I'm planning to call some of the patients and follow up."

"Don't you give your phone number to some?"

"Sure, and you know how often that works. Most have adopted a clinic mentality where the primary relationship is patient-clinic, not patient-doctor, even if I'm the only one that sees them. They also don't want to disturb me at home, even if they wind up in a red light to the ER. It's a hard pattern to break."

"The patients got along before you came to the clinic and I strongly suspect they can survive without you for two weeks."

"I'm not so sure, but I hope I was of some use."

4 p.m. Wednesday

"So Dad, how was it being home for the second day?"

"The morning was about as miserable as the first. I can do just so much laundry and re-straightening of my room. I made my follow-up phone calls and one old fellow was not doing so well, so I made a house call." He braced for a cyclone as the words exited his mouth.

"You did what? Riding around in not so good neighborhoods—you've got to admit that's where many of your patients live. Do you even know your way around?"

"They have this thing, Google Maps, fantastic, takes all the guesswork out of navigation. You just put..."

"I know how Google Maps works. What I'm having trouble with is a seventy-six year old man with a medical bag going into unsavory neighborhoods. You might as well have a "Mug Me" sign on your back."

"Nobody bothered me. And it's a good thing I made the visit. The poor guy was slipping into congestive heart failure. He wouldn't leave his house so I gave him a shot of lasix, a diuretic and a few other pills to slow his heart rate and strengthen his pump. It should let him get by without a stay in the hospital."

"Promise me you won't do the Marcus Welby thing and drive around that neighborhood again."

"But a sick man can't wait until our paint dries. And he is sure as hell not going to drive across town to sit for a couple of hours before being seen at the University Hospital clinic."

"Dad, you're my responsibility. Mom made me promise to watch after you, and that's what I'm doing. Please, please, please, no more house calls. Promise me."

"I promise I won't do house calls without telling you or Marta exactly where I'll be. How's that?"

"Not good enough. You will make me miss my classes, because I'm going with you."

"Oh come on Suzie, that's silly."

"No sillier than you putting your life in danger. Have you watched the evening news lately?"

"I know you're only saying this because you love me. I'll have to think of another way."

7 a.m. Friday

"Dad why are you dressed like a doctor?"

"Because I am one and I'm going off to fight disease and suffering."

"You promised no house calls. Do I have to call school and say I'm sick so I can go with you?"

"No house calls."

"Then where are you off to, and what is that smile about?"

"I'm off to the clinic."

"But that won't be ready for at least another couple of weeks. You told me they found even more dry rot."

"Not the old clinic, the new one."

"What's going on? Did someone donate a new clinic while I wasn't looking?"

"Well....Yes....I did."

"What? You know your pension has to last the rest of your life, which could be a decade or two given your family history. Did someone talk you into donating some huge amount? The county should be paying..."

"Relax, I just rented a clinic. Actually the shape of the old clinic gave me the idea. It looks like a railroad car, or the cheaper version, a trailer. And as luck may have it there are lots full of trailers for sale...or rent. It was delivered last night. Turns out the Mayor is on our Board of Directors. When he called, our landlord was more than happy to let us park the trailer in one corner of the parking lot. It's not as if there are huge crowds waiting to visit our neighbor, the payday lender."

"How are you and Marcey going to fit?"

"We've been talking that over. Marcey had the idea to put a couple of benches which the county will donate, outside with an awning for shade. Then her patients come in the front and mine in the back. The Mayor is so proud of this he invited Channel 6 to cover our first day. He says this is the 'can do' spirit that his administration fosters, or some other 're-elect me' phrase."

"Why did I ever doubt you'd find a way, Dad!"

CHAPTER 20

A SUIT FOR DOC PART 1

"Mrs. Jackson, I'd be glad to discuss your husband's condition. Cal is a sick man. All those years of smoking have made his lungs look like Swiss cheese; in medical terms he has emphysema," said Doc into the office phone.

"How bad is it? What can you do to make him well? You know he was such a strong man. He could do the work of three of those summer teenagers who fill in at the warehouse. Tell me what he should take and I'll make sure he does."

"He has severe emphysema. Our tests show his lung function is less than 20% of what it should be. I can't repair the holes in his lung, but I can give him medicine to help clear any mucus and to open up his bronchial tubes a bit. He's too old for a lung transplant..."

"Transplant? Are you kidding me? We came to you for a tune up, not to rip out the whole engine."

"I'm just listing the possible ways to help people with Cal's type of lung condition. First we'll get him a couple of inhalers, which you can pick up here so they won't cost you anything. We'll apply to the county for a nebulizer, a machine that makes a medicated mist that Cal should inhale three times a day. And he must, must, must stop every puff of every cigarette."

"How about switching to a pipe or cigars?"

"He shouldn't inhale anything unless it contains medicine to open up his bronchial tubes. Any kind of smoke stops his natural defenses from cleaning out the bronchial tubes."

"What did his X-ray show?"

"Lots of emphysema, lots of scarring. It's an old machine, but still gives us a pretty good picture of what's there. I can send Cal to the University for a new computerized chest x-ray and if that shows anything we could do a C-T scan."

"No way. He can't walk half a block. How is he going to make it around University Hospital? Its two blocks from the parking deck to registration. And we're not wasting a whole day just for a newer picture that will show the same old thing."

"I understand your position. If you'd rather not go, be sure he uses those inhalers just as I prescribed. He can take an extra two puffs if he is really short of breath, but no more than every four hours. And I need to see him back in two weeks."

3 months later

"Hello Mrs. Jackson, glad you called. I was wondering what happened to Cal. He was supposed to see me a long time ago. How is he doing? In the hospital? Why?"

"They think he has lung cancer. And they say he's in no shape for an operation. They want to look down his bronchial tubes to see if it's malignant or not. What should I do?"

"I think you should tell Cal that we need to know what's going on in his lungs, and if the University specialists want to look down his bronchial tubes, he ought to let them."

"Well OK Doc, if you say so."

"And please call me once you know more."

1 week later

A tearful voice greeted Doc, "He's in the ICU with a tube down his throat. They hooked him up to a machine and don't know if he'll be able to breathe without it."

"Tell me what happened. Did they do the bronchoscopy?"

"Just like you told me, and right after that they said he wasn't breathing good enough and they put down that goddam tube. It's driving him nuts. He coughs all the time and keeps reaching for it, so they had to tie his hands down and sedate him more. He's so miserable. What are we going to do?"

"And what about the results of the bronchoscopy?"

She started to sob. "He's got lung cancer, and it's bad, all the way up his bronchial tubes on one side. They say he's too sick for any treatment. Can you talk to them? Maybe there's something they'll tell you they won't tell me."

"Sure, I'll call as soon as we hang up and get right back to you."

9 a.m. Next Day

"Doc, you've got a call."

"I'm so sorry to take so long to get back with you. We had a whole family who inhaled carbon monoxide from a leaky space heater. We had ambulances here all day. When I called the ICU they were all busy with an emergency. I was just about to call them back."

"Well don't bother. The emergency was my Cal. The machine blew a hole in his lung. They worked on him for over an hour, putting a tube into his chest, doing CPR. He died. HE DIED. MY CAL IS DEAD!"

"I'm so sorry Mrs. Jackson. Is there anything I can do?"

"You've done enough. He was sick when I came to see you, but he was alive. You said we should do that procedure. You know what one resident said? He said that you should have seen the cancer on a chest x-ray, that's what he said."

"It's impossible to see a tumor through all the scarring on his x-ray. And besides, he wasn't a candidate for surgery."

"He might-a-been if you had seen it earlier. There was that x-ray from when Cal saw the other doctor who moved up north. I think both of you missed it."

"I'm so sorry for your loss. I will pull out the x-rays and look at them again. I'll call you after I do."

"Like you called me back last time? Don't bother, you can tell it to my lawyer. He says I've got a case. I was so lucky to meet him in the hospital cafeteria; otherwise I never would have believed I could afford one."

When she hung up, the telephone's click was like a slap. He knew that sick feeling in his chest–the same as anytime he had not done his homework, had disappointed a parent, had let down those who trusted him. As a thousand thoughts wrestled for his attention, his body made it to the box that served as their x-ray file. He pulled the file of Jackson, Cal, holding each up to the light box in turn. Emphysema was undeniable, large holes in the upper lung zones; increased lung markings from chronic bronchitis, the footprints of the Marlboro man having visited often; but no tumor was apparent— none that an unbiased observer could call.

An unbiased observer? Courts were full of experts, but unbiased wasn't one of the attributes prized by plaintiff's lawyers.

Doc could hear the howling of the jackals just out of sight, waiting to feast on his bones.

CHAPTER 21

A SUIT FOR DOC PART 2

Doc approached the attractive young woman who sat beneath the gilded sign 'McDonald, Cummings and Vanderhoff, Attorneys at Law'.

"How can I help you?" she said with a smile.

"Mr. McDonald represents the County and therefore the Free Clinic and its medical staff, so I guess that makes him my attorney. I have a 10 a.m. appointment."

Thirty minutes later

"I've been looking at magazines for the past half hour. Do you have WIFI in this office that I may use?"

"Of course we do, it's unlocked, but please come in Doctor, he can see you now."

Doc walked into a room that could have been the lobby of a Ritz-Carlton hotel. The office was as upscale as any Doc had seen. One wall was covered with river rock, a cascade of light blue water making the stones sparkle. The chair embraced him in the softest leather ever created.

Doc vowed to ask for the manufacturer when this was over, though he knew he couldn't afford even one ottoman.

Behind a large mahogany desk, polished so that Doc imagined he could see the attorney's face in duplicate, sat Mr. Laughton Wainwright McDonald lll. He sprung from behind the desk. His suit was tan to match his skin tone and cut like a second skin. He was polished, trim and as alert as a cheetah on the prowl.

"Have a seat, Doctor," he said thrusting out a hand but modulating the grip like he would for a woman, thought Doc. The implication that he was fragile and needed careful handling rankled to his core.

"Just call me Doc."

"And please call me Wain. Only my mother called me Laughton, and that was when I was in trouble."

"Speaking of that, am I in trouble?" asked Doc.

"In a word, no."

"Then why am I here?"

"You are being sued for malpractice, but the county will cover all costs as long as you agree to co-operate in a joint defense."

"Why wouldn't I?"

"No reason. We're on the same side of the table."

"But I haven't been served with any papers yet."

"I know, but you will be, this afternoon. We have some friends at the courthouse and the papers are being filed right now. I'd like you to look them over and call me if you see any factual errors, large or small."

"What's the next step?"

"They will find a hired gun, probably a university professor who wants to make $750 an hour to review records and testify that black is white."

"There was no tumor visible on the x-rays."

"Tumor or no tumor is less important to me than potential damages. We'll argue that it was not gross negligence, so it's covered under Sovereign immunity, limits of liability $100,000 by state law."

"But it does matter to me. I did nothing wrong. I've practiced for over forty years and was never sued before. It's important that you believe me."

"It's not what I believe, but what the jury finds, if we get that far. Remember Doc, this is not your dime we're spending."

"But it is my reputation."

"So they won't hire you for a tenured position?" he said laughing. "I think that ship has sailed...no offense."

Doc left more discomfited than when he entered. A process server was waiting at the clinic and handed Doc a large brown envelope, which he set aside.

"Reading material?" said Marcey. "I guess that means I eat lunch alone."

"I've got no appetite anyway."

"Don't get yourself into a twist over this Doc. Malpractice suits are a cottage industry at the University Hospital. Most go nowhere."

"Let's hope you're right."

Marcey brought in a sandwich and could hear Doc's voice through the closed door. "Didn't properly examine, what the hell... mumble, mumble. Didn't take a history...."

"Are you OK Doc?"

"Do you know what those lying SOBs said in official court documents? They said I didn't..."

"I heard, through the door. That's what they say in every case, but proving it is another matter."

"But my reputation..."

"Doc, I know how you love statistics. Here's one: more than half of all primary care physicians, low risk specialists, have been sued and many, more than once. Twenty percent of all neurosurgeons are sued each year."

"Thanks but I still feel like a guy who's been mugged."

That night was spent on the computer looking up anything he could find on the dreaded topic of malpractice.

"What are you so busy doing Dad? Got a big problem case?" said Suzie.

"Don't be so glib. What I do is important and I do it well," he nearly shouted.

"Whoa, what's going on? Since when do you bring problems home and shout at me? Even Marta said you were a 'grunon', a grumpy old bear."

"Watch the 'old', but I do apologize. This poor lady just lost her husband, so I can't be angry at her just because some predator with a law degree ambushed her at the hospital and convinced her that we, that I, committed malpractice by missing the diagnosis of a tumor that wasn't there on two x-rays from the clinic, a tumor that could not be treated because of this poor man's end stage lung disease, and the poor guy suffered because of complications of a procedure that I told her it was OK to proceed with because doctors have to have faith in each other, and one jerky resident implanted the notion that I missed an x-ray finding probably to deflect blame since he felt bad that the patient was failing and now with all the ethical lawyers in the state, I've got to deal with a bantam rooster of an attorney who doesn't give a damn about the truth, just how much money he can save the county and I don't trust him further than I can throw his Mercedes."

"Take a breath Dad. I can see that this is really rocking you. Seriously now, is it worth it?"

"I never thought I'd say it, but I'm not sure. I'll go through with this charade, this insulting charade, but I may need some protection of my own."

One week later at law office

"Hey Doc, thanks for coming to my shop. We've signed up the chief of internal medicine at Yale and the head of Johns Hopkins radiology who will swear on a stack of bibles that there is no tumor to be seen on the x-ray. By the way, you do have the old x-ray from a year ago, don't you?" As he spoke he closed the massive door to his office." It's too bad that x-ray exists because another radiologist could say there was a change from the old one to the new one. It might earn them some points with the jury. It would remove the last shred of doubt if that film wasn't at trial, if it was misplaced."

"Doc could feel the heat in his face before the words formed on his lips. "You're asking me to lose the x-rays?"

"Just between you and me and these four walls, yes, but you know I would NEVER tell a client to do anything illegal," he said with a smirk. And I don't need to remind you that the county will cover your liability, IF you cooperate with the defense. I'm not feeling a whole lot of cooperation here."

"So you are telling me that if I don't 'lose' the x-ray that you won't defend me?"

"I don't need to tell you that life is full of hard choices Doc."

"You, Laughton Wainwright McDonald lll are absolutely right."

'What?..." began the attorney as he viewed Doc through squinting eyelids. Doc pulled the pen he had gotten from the Spy shop for $109.99 on sale. He pushed the 'send' button, twisted the cap and heard the unmistakably overconfident sneer of his attorney who made a lunge for the pen just as Doc pulled it away and tucked it into his side pocket.

"You know this has been transmitted over your WIFI to a recorder outside this building."

"You sneaky old bastard. How dare you. I'm the one who is going to keep you from the wolves."

"And I'm the one who is going to keep you from the bar association, if and only if you play this one straight down the middle. No lost x-rays, no altered medical records. There are enough facts here to win the case as is. So do your job and we'll both wind up blameless."

2 months later

"Hey Doc," said Marcey with a big smile, "You've got a call from Mr. McDonald's secretary," as she handed the phone to Doc.

"They dropped the case?" said Doc. That's great news. Why?"

"The other attorney wasn't willing to keep laying out money for expert witnesses after the first set told him there was really nothing on the x-rays. Mrs. Jackson was more than willing to throw in the towel. She felt she had done all she could to defend poor Cal." Doc thanked the secretary and exhaled his relief.

"So Doc how does it feel to have this behind you?" said Marcey.

"You know the old joke about why people bang their heads against the wall? Because it feels so good when they stop. That's sort of how I feel."

"Are you ready to jump back into the clinic routine?"

Like the first day, he weighed several answers then said, "You bet."

CHAPTER 22

ON THE PRECIPICE

Doc was there early Friday morning but noted the lights were already on. He entered to find Marcey, eyes red and swollen. "What's the matter?" he asked.

"They're closing the clinic," she managed, while working hard to restrain a torrent of tears.

"Why?"

"They say the money could be used more efficiently at the county hospital."

"But that's twenty miles away, an hour in rush hour traffic. It makes no sense. Where did you hear of this ridiculous idea?"

"I got this email last night after the county commissioners meeting." Doc took the paper by one corner as if it were evidence at a crime scene. He read it carefully.

"It says we have till the end of the month. That's something."

"I've been told by my boss, the head of nursing at the county hospital, that if I make a fuss I'm gone, along with most of my pension," said Marcey.

"We still have some time. This isn't over by a long shot," said Doc.

They slogged through the day, putting on the best faces possible. When Doc saw Bill and Helen in follow up, they immediately sensed that something was wrong. Bill knew one of the county commissioners from the Rotary Club and said he would call her as soon as he got home.

Politics had never been to Doc's liking. He always thought that a little power or the desire to keep it brought out the worst in many people—not all but many. Through his career he had served on the committees he must, but steadfastly refused to run for Chief of the Medical Executive Committee.

"You've got the perfect personality to foster compromise." But Doc knew that such a position meant taking a stand on issues that affected the income of his colleagues such as who took ER call in orthopedics or who had prime blocks of OR time. It was a snake pit and having supportive colleagues or not, Doc knew the best anti-venom was not to put your foot in at all.

"How have you avoided being Chief all these years?" asked other doctors.

"Allergies," responded Doc. "I'm allergic to hospital politics."

Bill called that night and said the vote to close the clinic was four in favor and three opposed. His friend, the commissioner, who supported the clinic, was incensed. The county hospital wasted money as if it printed hundred dollar bills, which it nearly did. There was a half cent sales tax that went to provide county-wide health services. Still with all the hospital vice-presidents, department administrators and consultants, there never seemed to be enough money to go round.

Doc sat down with a large yellow pad, his favorite tool for analyzing difficult issues. He drew a line down the center of the page.

On the left he listed all the problems:

1. No money for the clinic
2. No local care for those who need it the most
3. Insufficient public awareness
4. Insufficient public support for the clinic
5. Insufficient political support

To the right of the line Doc wrote. "Appear before the Board at next week's meeting." Doc knew he was stepping into the snake pit alone, for Marcey couldn't risk her pension and her job. Doc also knew he had one thing in his favor. Just as age was often accompanied by physical dependence, it was often accompanied by social and financial independence. He had no paying job to lose. There was no mortgage on his home and a social security check would continue to arrive in the second week of each month, clinic or no clinic. He doodled in the margins 'Annis Veniet Cum Robore' a phrase he had come across years ago that seemed to be emblazoned on his battle flag, 'With Years Comes Strength'.

Doc prepared for the meeting as he would for a grand rounds presentation. Each fact was crosschecked and carefully documented. He edited the presentation down to the fifteen minutes he was allotted. He had charts showing how many patients visited the clinic and as that number increased their utilization of the ER decreased by 60%. Doc listed the cost per uninsured patient visit at the clinic. He wasn't sure what the cost was per ER visit, but he did know that no bill started at less than $250, plus a la carte charges thereafter.

Suzie and Marta joined Marcey at the council meeting. When Doc's turn to speak came up, the head of the City Council iinterrupted him. "Since the agenda is so full, outside speakers will have only five minutes. Three commissioners spoke in protest of this last minute decision, labeled arbitrary and high handed, to no avail. Doc was rattled. So this was how the opposition was silenced these days. Doc edited on the fly, discussed the clinic savings and offered to submit backup for the record. He pointed out that acute care an hour away was no longer acute care. He pointed out that voters had supported access to community care on their bond referendum, not an ever enlarging public hospital. When he finished, it was to applause, and not just from his family and friends.

A re-vote was requested but the results were the same. The Chairman moved onto a discussion of free mammograms at the hospital.

The four were discouraged as they sat in the coffee shop around the corner. "Don't give up," said Doc.

"We'll figure something out. If routine therapy doesn't work, then sometimes a more radical approach is needed."

"Short of self-immolation—which I am NOT recommending—how can you get the public to care about one small community clinic?" said Marcey.

"They say sunshine is the best disinfectant," said Doc. "Let's test out that theory."

At Monday's clinic session Doc was met by cameras from all the local TV stations and CNN. Walking around the clinic were clusters of people carrying signs. One offered a poster to Doc who took it with a big smile and merged in an endless counterclockwise circle. He even joined in with the chant:

"Hey, hey, ho, ho, our neighborhood clinic cannot go. Ho, ho, hey, hey, our neighborhood clinic has to stay." The people had come in response to Doc's letter to the editor of Sunday's paper. It reviewed the reasons for the clinic's continued existence. The editor had added to the pressure with a whole column about local, not centralized health care delivery. They had focused on pre-natal care, which was much more effective when pregnant patients didn't have to take two buses to get to the hospital OB department.

Thanks to Suzie and her computer skills there was also a crowd funding program to raise money, awareness and perhaps, to embarrass the chairman of the City Council.

A long black limousine arrived and the chairman stepped out with a proclamation endorsing the clinic and praising all those who worked there. He stood next to Doc facing the TV cameras and said, "We on the Council have re-evaluated priorities, done some creative accounting, and after a late night session, we found the money for the clinic to stay open."

Doc listened then added:

"Since the council agrees with our model of delivering community centered health care, the clinic system should be expanded all through our city, with local medical services available in each neighborhood."

The chairman fumphered, turned a bit red and said, "Of course we will take that under advisement."

CHAPTER 23

COMPANY

Doc found himself facing each week with optimism and anticipation, in no small measure because of the Wednesday night canasta games, the talk with his friends the Gordon's and especially his partner Julia; perhaps in no small measure because she seemed delighted to be there, to be in his presence.

"This is silly," thought Doc, "unseemly for a man my age; for God's sake. It's bordering on disloyalty to Roberta's memory. I'll have to make it clear that we're just playing cards, and it can't go any further. What would Suzie say?"

The usual Wednesday crowd filled half a dozen tables, some with pleasant banter, some with silent concentration. When break time came, Doc went for the coffee and biscotti and found Julia next to him.

"Doc, can I talk to you away from the group?" His own private hurricane warnings went off in his head, but were overruled by the manners many are taught, some at med school in Richmond, some in church, some on the street corners of Brooklyn—'First do no harm', 'treat others as you would like to be treated', 'don't be a jerk… unless absolutely necessary.'

"Sure, there's a couch out in the hallway."

"I'll go first, and you can follow in a couple of minutes," said Julia. "I don't want too many tongues wagging."

"Ah, stealth, a specialty of mine," said Doc. She giggled and Doc felt a warmth come over him. He followed instructions and resisted the impulse to keep checking his watch. He did have to beg off a conversation about one player's gall bladder, promising to get back to him later in the evening.

Julia was sitting at one end of a three person couch and Doc took the other, putting his coffee cup next to hers on the cocktail table. He waited. This was her meeting.

"Doc, I really like coming here on Wednesday nights. I like spending time with the Gordon's and I really like spending time with you."

"Let me say.." said Doc.

Julia continued: "This is hard for me so please let me finish, then I promise I'll listen." He nodded.

"When Stuart died two years ago I didn't want to live. Our kids are grown and scattered. For the past year I've made myself go out, to the theater, or a museum, or lunch. Coming here was a big step. What's missing is someone to share these activities. Don't panic, I'm not looking for another husband and Stuart and I saved our money so I have more than enough...I'm not looking for financial security. I like your company. You're kind and funny and not full of yourself. You'd be surprised how many people don't fit those simple criteria. I'd like to spend more time with you." She exhaled a sigh laden with doubt and fears of rejection. "Does this shock you?"

"Shock me? Not even a little bit. I was just saying to myself that I look forward to canasta, even though I'm not much for cards. I do enjoy your company and you are a primary reason I keep coming back, but it's complicated. I was busy studying to get into medical school and didn't go out much. Roberta and I dated in college and we were in our twenties when we got married. I took the 'till death do you part' seriously and we were married just over fifty years. She was the love of my life. We two and Suzie were a unit, an unbreakable unit. It seems so disloyal, unfaithful to be spending time with another woman. I wouldn't know how."

"I don't want to replace your wife. I don't want you to replace my Stuart. It seems to me that we got the long straw and have outlived our partners. We can spend that time alone, in perpetual mourning or we can find someone to share our remaining days, to infuse laughter, to appreciate and be appreciated. I'm sorry for being so forward, but I don't know how much time either of us has, and keeping these thoughts to myself doesn't seem like a winning strategy."

"What would my daughter say? Would she be upset? I'm just not sure. You know, I'm not a young man, Julia. I'm seventy-six."

"I know, and I'll be seventy in November. How about we do this," said Julia." I have two tickets to a musical at the Broward Center for Saturday night. We could have dinner and see the show. No commitments other than one evening. However it turns out, we have to promise to keep playing canasta on Wednesday nights."

"I'll have to talk to my daughter first. It's a conversation I'm not looking forward to, and then I'll call."

"Fair enough. We'd best get back before they think we've been kidnapped."

"Enough stealth for one evening," said Doc. "Let's walk back together."

For the first time since they sat, Julia smiled.

Thursday Evening

"Suzie, I need to talk to you about something."

"Uh oh. That's the voice when I didn't do my homework."

"Relax you're off the hook. I'm the one with a problem. You know Julia, the lady I play canasta with?"

"It's OK Dad."

"I didn't say anything yet."

"I know, but I've been waiting a long time for this conversation."

"She wants to go out to the theater and dinner, and I'm not sure what's right, if it's disloyal to Mom's memory. How would you feel?"

"Mom didn't want you to be alone. 'People need people' is what she told me. It would have been really uncomfortable if I went around trying to set you up, so I've stayed out of it. But people *do* need people. Maybe that's why I stumbled prematurely into my short lived marriage."

"I'm glad you understand," said Doc.

"You know Dad, I haven't gone on lots of dates but I think we both deserve a second chance. There is a really nice English Lit teacher at my school named Roger who asked me out, and I think I'll say yes. No double dating with my father, though, that would be really strange... at least at first."

CHAPTER 24

ON BOARD

"Doc, they want you to serve on the Board," said Marcey.

"Who are they and what Board are they talking about?"

"The Community Health Board. It has members of all groups providing health care in the city: the hospital, each of the community outreach centers and the Mayor, who is the chairman. The one unrepresented is our little free clinic. The hospital administrator said we should have a presence, if only to know which way the wind is blowing, especially if it's a hurricane force gale."

"And you don't want this honor?"

"You know Brent and I have our wedding to plan. Also our prenatal clinic will be extra busy now that the hospital is limiting their OB clinic to four days a week. It would be a way for you to make contact with some of the movers and shakers in the community."

"Somehow I've managed to get through all these years without being either a mover or a shaker. And you know I hate committee meetings, they're so dull and expensive."

"Expensive?" asked Marcey.

"Take the hourly wages of each of the committee members times the number of hours of the meeting and sometimes it's a pretty astounding number. If people realized the cost they wouldn't talk so much, they'd stick to the agenda and actually accomplish something."

"That is exactly the practical attitude they need at the Board meeting. So what do you say?"

"I'll agree to sit in on one meeting and then decide. No commitment. When is the next meeting?"

"Tonight at 8."

"Thanks for giving me some time to get dinner."

Doc arrived early, was given a copy of the twelve item agenda and a list of names of prospective attendees. Five minutes before the meeting the Mayor came in flanked by two aides. He was all smiles and after one aide whispered in his ear, he strode over to Doc, hand extended.

"Hello, I'm Mayor Davidson; you must be the new doctor from the Free Clinic. Welcome to the trenches." Doc shook the Mayor's warm soft hand.

"Please call me Doc. I'm just observing; haven't signed on officially yet."

"Well I hope you do. That fine clinic of yours needs a seat at the table." And his attention was already elsewhere before the warmth of his handshake could cool.

Doc had time to chat with the city hospital administrator, the one person in the room who could improve care for his patients. Her name tag announced that she was an RN, BSN, MBA and some other initials that Doc didn't recognize, probably having to do with professional societies. They had spoken in the past when Doc needed a patient admitted who was clearly sick enough to be in the hospital, but didn't fall into one of the payment buckets that opened the ER door. She had the remnants of a Jamaican accent and had generally been helpful, if a bit formal. Doc hoped that putting his face to an anonymous voice might smooth the way in the future.

The agenda began with budgets, catchment areas and algorithms for where ambulances delivered sick patients. Doc quickly realized that most of the people in the room were community representatives who eyed each other with suspicion, protecting what little privilege they had against others, often of a different skin shade or language. Many of the rest were administrators, whose strong suit was not clinical medicine. In fact, Doc and the head of the hospital ER were the only practicing physicians in the room. There was one nurse, the hospital administrator—a non-practicing RN—and a pharmacist.

The fourth item on the agenda was "Pregnant women; when is transfer to hospital necessary?" This devolved into a shouting match between Jose Delgado, a farm worker who recounted that his cousin had not been sent from a clinic to the hospital for third trimester bleeding. Alfred Haley, a well known black activist stood and yelled back: "The County shouldn't waste money on people who aren't here legally."

"Our people pay taxes and my brother is in the Marines, so don't you go tellin' me about supporting this country," Delgado countered. "How many of your people even work, let alone pay taxes?"

"First you take the jobs then you tell me we don't pay taxes," said Haley who stormed across the room as Delgado lifted a folding chair.

Doc now knew why the two uniformed police officers were in the room. They quickly placed themselves between the two charging bulls and ended a scene that Doc was sure would have resulted in bloodshed. Like boxers, separated by a referee, the combatants glared at each other but eventually went back to neutral corners. Those who had moved to safer ground returned to their seats. The noise evaporated like morning mist and the imminent brawl became a meeting once again. The Mayor, apparently used to such disarray went back to item four of the agenda. Now it was each faction hurling angry questions, accusations, and insults at the hospital administrator for not providing care to those most vulnerable. After several minutes, Doc asked for permission to speak. The Mayor was thrilled to get the discussion on a different track.

"The medical issue here is clear. A patient with third trimester bleeding should be seen by a medical care provider. In our center that is a nurse practitioner who knows a lot more about prenatal care than I do." At this the administrator smiled. "The problem is where to deliver the care," Doc continued. "We are all being squeezed by budgetary constraints, so the hospital, the final backstop for the poor of our community, is being forced to limit prenatal clinic hours to four days a week. This means that almost half the time those vital services are not available. It is not the clinic's fault, or the hospital's fault. We all depend on the local government to fund services so the good people in the clinics and hospitals can do their jobs and provide first class care despite a patient's ability to pay.

The solution Mr. Mayor is in your hands. Help us all by finding the funding to keep the hospital's OB clinics open seven days a week." All further comments were drowned out by applause and loud cries of approval in several different languages. The Mayor who had been engrossed in his email looked shocked as he turned for orientation from his aides. After a period of back and forth with his Chief of Staff, the Mayor looked up and said: "Will someone put that in the form of a motion, so I can bring it to our budgetary meeting Monday? If this is the unanimous vote of the committee, I'm sure we can move some funding around. No promises but I'm reasonably certain we can make this happen. Why don't you make the motion Doc?"

"I'm not even on the committee yet, so perhaps the administrator of our municipal hospital should make it." She did and after a brief squabble between Delgado and Haley over who would second the motion, both did, it passed unanimously. The rest of the meeting was a blur of issues that were dealt with in a spirit of cooperation.

"Doc that was spectacular," said the hospital administrator. "I've been trying to get that funding for the past six months. Well done. And by the way, my name is Gloria. Call me any time if you need something. I do hope you decide to join the Board. It's good to have the voice of someone who has experience living in the real world."

"So, Doc, I hear you hit a home run, first time up at bat," said Marcey.

"Just lucky, but I don't think I can take those meetings."

"Too dull?"

"No, not dull enough."

CHAPTER 25

PEER REVIEW

"Hey Doc, I've got a huge favor to ask. Could you cover my practice next weekend?" said Dr. John Stevens, an internist Doc had known for thirty years. "My grandson is graduating from high school and I shouldn't miss it; I can't miss it. I leave Friday and will be back Sunday night."

"I'd love to help you out John, but it's been years since I did hospital practice. What about the guys you normally cross cover with?"

"They're either retired or taking call for their own limited practices."

"I don't have any malpractice insurance that covers hospital care. Don't forget, I was retired for many years before I started back at the free clinic eight months ago. I'm not the guy you want."

"You are exactly who I want. We both have a few years on us, and I'd hate to turn over the practice to some kid who was a junior resident last week. The hospital has full time primary care guys to take care of any of my folks who get admitted. I just need someone to handle phone calls and see patients for a couple of hours each morning in my office. I can even have you hired as a locum tenens by a physician locator firm, and I'll pay them for your services. That way they provide you with malpractice insurance. You're already licensed in this State so the paperwork will be easy. You charge for whatever you do, my office can bill and reimburse you when we get paid."

"I'm not interested in getting paid. If I do this it would be one time only, to help out an old colleague, an old friend. There is one thing: would you be willing to help out the clinic on my days off if they have a problem patient?"

"Absolutely."

"You're working weekends now?" said Suzie. "You've got to be kidding. Having no time off to rest was one of the things that made you retire, remember?"

"What could I do? I've known John forever and he has nowhere else to turn."

"Where would he turn when you collapse from exhaustion?"

"It's only a couple of hours for two days, that's all."

"Until he calls again, asking you to cross cover."

"No chance. I made that clear."

Saturday Morning 9 a.m.

"Hello Mrs. Adorno, I'm covering for Doctor Stevens. What seems to be the problem?"

"I have itching that Dr. Stevens says is due to chronic dermatitis."

"How long have you had this?"

"Two years, but it's been a lot worse the past month."

"Are you using any new soap, shampoo, perfume, doing any gardening, any new medications or vitamins?"

"No...No to all."

"Any other symptoms?"

"Well I have had nausea and some weight loss; that and the annoying back pain."

"What did Dr, Stevens say about these complaints?"

"Each time I reminded him of my problems he'd say: 'What do you expect at your age?'"

Doc went through a review of systems, asking questions touching upon the major organ systems. When he examined the patient and pushed with his thumb on her ankles, a deep imprint remained.

"You seem to have some fluid in your legs. Have you noticed it before?"

"I pointed it out to Dr. Stevens months ago. He said a woman my age frequently retains fluid. 'It's hormonal' were his exact words."

"I don't see any blood work on the chart."

"I asked about that. He said there was so much unnecessary testing in this country that it was going to drive us all into bankruptcy. He said he would order any tests I needed individually, but not those multitest panels."

"I think that now is the time to get some of those tests to make sure that your kidneys are working well, or that there is not another underlying cause for all your symptoms." Doc filled out forms for a chemistry panel, CBC and urinalysis and had his nurse set up an appointment at the local Quest Lab.

The next patient wanted a prescription for a three month supply of oxycontin for chronic back pain. When Doc suggested a consult with a pain specialist the patient stormed out saying: "I'll wait for Dr. Stevens."

The third patient was brought in by his wife after he nearly passed out when standing from the kitchen table. He was on three different medications for high blood pressure including a strong diuretic.

"Have you had dizziness before?" asked Doc.

"For months but Dr. Stevens wants my blood pressure to be normal so I don't have a stroke."

"In what position does he check your blood pressure, lying, sitting, standing perhaps?"

"His nurse checks it sitting and one time when I nearly passed out in the office she checked it with me lying down."

Doc determined that the neurological exam was normal. He then checked the blood pressure with the patient sitting...120/80 and standing...90/60. The patient swayed and had to be helped into a sitting position.

"Your blood pressure drops when you stand, meaning that you need less medication."

"Nurse, would you get Mr. Hollings some salty soup and crackers."

"And you sir should stop taking the water pill, it's making you dehydrated. We'll be back to check your blood pressure again in twenty minutes."

Doc found three other patients who had been wrongly diagnosed or treated. He thought he would be angry but felt only sadness. When Sunday night came, he called Dr. Stevens who was ebullient. "Can't thank you enough Doc. What a fabulous weekend. Any of my old biddies give you trouble?"

"Let me come by tomorrow and we'll go over a couple of charts."

"Thanks a million for the coverage, but I don't think there's any reason to trouble yourself and come all the way over here."

"I've done it for two days, so one more won't make a difference. I'll be there at 9," then he hung up before further objections could be offered.

Monday 9 a.m.

Doc couldn't understand it. John had trained at prestigious university hospitals. He was an astute physician, or had been. When Doc saw his old friend come in, he understood.

Dr. Stevens entered slowly. His gait was uncoordinated, hands moved with sudden jerky motions and there were disquieting facial grimaces. He would occasionally make a grunting sound that he tried to cover by pretending to cough.

"How long?"asked Doc.

"About a year now, but I am managing. I'm on an experimental protocol from the University's neurology clinic. They say it's Huntington's disease."

"What about your son Jack? It's caused by a dominant genetic defect, as I recall."

"In fifty percent, but thankfully he has no signs of it."

"How do you examine patients?"

"My nurse does that for me."

"Does she also fill out prescriptions?"

"She has to. My shaky handwriting is unreadable."

Doc went over each case. In each instance Dr.Stevens had an excuse for missing the diagnosis.

"John, you are clearly not functioning well. Do you remember what was wrong with Mr. Hollings?"

"What difference does that make? His chart is right here and I don't memorize each one, do you?"

"We just talked about him. We both know that Huntington's can be accompanied by memory loss."

"Are you saying I have dementia? How dare you!"

"John just humor me. Can you count backward from one hundred by sevens?"

"What the hell are you doing? I'm not the patient here.

I thank you for the coverage and I'll thank you to get the hell out of my office."

Doc left more depressed than he came. What options did he have? Report his colleague to the Medical Board and it would start an investigation which would end with the name Dr. John Stevens listed in the Medical Board newsletter under 'license revoked for substandard practice.' His friend did not deserve that after delivering high quality medical care for thirty years, but neither could Doc ignore what was going on. He did not sleep well.

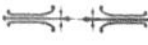

Wednesday 9 a.m.

The door opened to Dr. Stevens' waiting room. It was filled but not with patients. Seated next to Doc were Mrs. Stevens and their son, a pharmacist. There were also two other colleagues who had not retired but had stopped cross covering with John when they discovered subtle changes in the quality of his medical care.

"What's going on? Where are my patients?"

"Dad, we need to talk," said his son. "We're all concerned about you and the level of medical care you are providing. I've noted that you are more and more forgetful. Your colleagues have noted serious problems with patient care. One way or another Dad, it's time to retire. The doctors here have covered for you and have seen the changes." All three doctors nodded.

"I'm sorry John but it's true," said Dr. Rothberg. "I've seen it for the past year and I regret that I didn't say something sooner."

"Dad, these doctors are your colleagues and friends, but they are obligated to notify the State Board if a practitioner falls below the community standard of care," he said, handing his father a copy of the State's medical ethics brochure.

"You can't do this to me. I'll call my lawyer."

"You'll do no such thing John," said his wife. "You never deliberately hurt a patient in thirty years and you are not going to start now. Look darling, we've talked about your memory. From what Doc says there is a big issue with delegating lots of things to the nurses. Listen to what these three doctors are saying. You are overlooking things which may have harmed patients and it's only going to get worse. This has got to stop now."

They went around the room, each apologizing but ending with, "It's time."

Two weeks later John called to tell Doc that he was selling his practice to one of those youngsters just out of residency, and told Doc: "There are no hard feelings."

"It's for the best," said Doc. "Medicine these days is a young man's game."

Neither completely believed that, but both were happy to pretend that they did.

CHAPTER 26

WAITING

Doc found himself in a room filled with seniors, at least half using a walker, cane or wheel chair. Everywhere were swollen legs and bandages stanching superficial ulcers, always a threat to leak. These were the outward manifestations of inner disarray.

The sign-in list was partially covering the names of those who had arrived before, providing the mirage of anonymity. This was the office of three cardiologists. Doc the retired internist and now a patient, awaited the senior partner who was a young recruit when he introduced himself all those years ago.

"Is this penance for what I put patients through?" thought Doc. He had long ago rationalized making people wait, telling them that he could not promise to be on time, because it was impossible to predict the length of the preceding appointment. All he could promise was to spend as much time with each patient as they needed—which did not always translate into as much time as they wanted; for some wanted to gossip, talk about their latest travel adventure, or to show pictures and brag about their grandchildren. Often these were the same people who complained about waiting for others. Most of those who were acutely ill did not complain and left satisfied that their concerns had been addressed. The follow-up visit when they were improved was another story—waiting caused moods laced with black clouds and medical discussions interrupted by reminders of places they needed to be.

A series of thoughts bubbled up from his vat of mixed emotions.

1. My time does not lose its value just because I am a patient and retired. It feels as if I am being disrespected and devalued by the assumption that only the physician's time has worth.
2. Why am I sitting here at 11:05 when my appointment was for 10? I know they occasionally double book time slots to fit in an acutely ill patient, or if someone doesn't show up or is late so the doctor isn't idle for fifteen minutes. So what if he is? He can answer some of the waiting phone calls and he won't be out of touch until the end of office hours.
3. In this age of technologic intrusion, so extensive that our location can be tracked at any moment,

why do we have to sit here in an overcrowded room, with an overly loud TV that is invariably tuned to some offensive news channel? Why couldn't we be called ten minutes before the doctor is ready to see us–even senior citizens carry cell phones—so we can sit in the downstairs cafeteria, get in our ten thousand steps in the hallway, listen to music in our cars, anything other than sitting in a crowded waiting room wondering why that man was called first, worried about losing our place?

The smart ones brought books, really thick books, and sweaters. Why are doctor's offices so cold? Are they trying to preserve patients like left over hamburger in a refrigerator? Was I even aware of the waiting room temperature in my office? The only time I stepped into my waiting room was to handle an emergency that usually began by maneuvering a patient to an exam room. Is this Doctor's Hell, where all sins committed against others are boomeranged?

Doc cringed when other patients, old enough to be grandparents to the seemingly teenaged medical assistants, were called by their first names. It seemed at least disrespectful and at worst demeaning. It seemed to infantilize those whose only sin was growing old and added the loss of status and respect to the inability to walk unassisted.

Eventually Doc was handed an electronic tablet in which he entered his name and social security number. "Is this necessary?" he asked the young lady behind the opaque, sliding glass. "Surely you have this information since I've been coming here for decades."

"You haven't been here for over six months and we are required to reconfirm all information." Doc wanted to ask: "Required by whom?" but could sense a brick wall coming and decided it would be easier to comply. He had read in the AARP bulletin that one of the most frequent sources of identity theft was medical offices. He considered leaving out the social security number but he knew they already had it, and refusing to enter it would result in a warning in red preventing him from proceeding. I guess you have to choose your battles, he thought.

Then came legions of inquiries about each organ system. He knew that the more questions asked, even if irrelevant to his high blood pressure, the higher the charge allowed by Medicare. At 76 he could honestly answer yes to almost every complaint except menstrual irregularities. He decided to answer 'Yes' only if the symptom caused him problems or needed medication; still that was a daunting array. When Doc listed his medications, generics all, he was assaulted with pop-up ads for the latest high priced pharmaceutical, always accompanied by smiling patients and families, delighted with Grandpa's newly controlled blood pressure. Now he understood who paid for the electronic devices.

He stopped and cringed when he heard his first name called by a somewhat impatient medical assistant. He was weighed in the hall, pockets full and shoes on. What good is that? he wondered.

"I can tell you what I weighed naked this morning."

"That won't be necessary," said the assistant. He was led to an examination room, where she took his blood pressure.

"Perhaps I should remove the sweater first?" he asked. Either she didn't hear or chose not to, stood to leave, and called over her shoulder: "The doctor will be here shortly."

More than all the experiences of medical school, from having blood drawn by a classmate, to passing a tube through his own nose and into his stomach, this was the most educational.

All doctors should be patients for a day, thought Doc.

Then he began to plan some changes for his clinic.

CHAPTER 27
THE COST OF A LIFE

Doc was in a dark mood. There seemed to be no options. He had seen the Morales family since his first week at the clinic. Jorge, the father, was a lifetime away from the teenager who ran with the infamous Los Hermanos gang and lived the street life he needed to survive in his native Honduras. He grew up doing farm work and it was natural that his first and only job since emigrating to the US was at the 'All Things Green' plant nursery. He could barely speak English before enrolling in the ESL night classes at JP Taravella High School. He studied as if his financial survival depended upon it, which in no small way it did. Now he could speak and understand his new language, but also could joke in English, an essential requirement if he was to be accepted and liked by those he worked with. His efforts were rewarded with a promotion to supervisor, not physically less demanding, but with a larger number on each pay check.

"Dok-tor, Hawehre yoo?" he said to a puzzled looking Doc, before breaking into a roaring laugh.

"I'm just messing with you, Doc. It's good to see you."

"Thank God, I thought you had a stroke and forgot all those English lessons."

"Did I really sound like that first guy?"

"You were close, but you sure did improve quickly. By the way, how are your girls doing?"

"The twins graduate high school this year, with really good grades. They're applying for scholarships already, and if that doesn't work, they can go to community college and eventually transfer over. One thing is for damned sure, they are not going to have hands looking like these." He held up his thickened palms with dirt so imbedded that no amount of washing could make them entirely clean.

"What brings you in today, Jorge?"

"Something is not right when I pee."

"Burning? Blood in the urine?" asked Doc.

"No nothing like that, it's just that my water is really dark. It was never that color before."

"Any other symptoms, like fatigue or loss of appetite?"

"Both, How did you know?"

"They often go together." Doc had already noted the slight yellow discoloration of Jorge's eyes.

"When you were a younger guy living the wild life, did you ever use IV drugs?"

"No, my older brother Alvaro OD'ed right before my eyes and I swore never to put that poison in my veins."

"How about tattoos?"

"Sure, all of us had them. That way everyone knew not to mess with us."

"Who did the tattooing?"

"We didn't even have money for rice and beans, so we couldn't pay some artist. We did the tattoos ourselves."

"Did you use sterile needles?"

"Sterile my ass. We passed em through a flame after a friend used them, then handed the needle to the next guy."

Doc waded through thirty minutes of questions and careful examination, then sat down with Mr. and Mrs. Morales. "I'm very concerned that you may have a chronic form of hepatitis C."

"But I never shot drugs."

"You did share needles though, and passing it through a flame is not the same as using a sterile one."

"Am I totally screwed? What do I do now?"

"We'll have to make sure that this has not progressed to cirrhosis, but most don't. The treatment for cirrhosis is getting a new liver, a transplant. More likely you have a form of chronic hepatitis, and there is some really good news on that front with only a small hitch."

"Right now I need the good news."

"If you are found to have chronic Hep C, there is a new medication, Harvoni, that cures it—did you hear that word, CURES it—in twelve weeks."

"That's great Doc, what's the hitch?"

"I'm glad you're seated. The drug costs a lot, and the clinic doesn't have the funding to buy the pills."

"How much is a lot, I can borrow a few bucks from my family, especially if it gets me better."

"More than one thousand dollars....a pill. You take one a day for twelve weeks. The bottom line is about ninety-four thousand dollars."

"Are you shittin' me? All my relatives put together don't have that amount to spare. I don't think they even earn that much. Which bank am I supposed to rob?"

"We're getting ahead of ourselves. First we need to know for sure if this is caused by hepatitis C and second if you are in the majority who don't have cirrhosis. We'll need to draw blood from Carmen as well. It's not likely that she got the virus from you, but it is possible."

"Just make sure she knows this isn't some VD, or I'll be in real trouble."

"It's not," said Doc. "I'm going to send you to see an old friend at the University Hospital GI clinic. We have a special arrangement with them. I'm guessing that they will ask you for permission to do a liver biopsy and you should say 'yes'. While you work on that end, I'll see what I can do about the cost."

"I think you got the harder job, Doc."

"Me too."

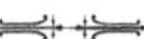

3 weeks later

"Well, as you know Jorge, your blood test did in fact show hepatitis C, with active virus still in your system. What you probably don't know is that the biopsy result came out today and shows chronic active hepatitis but no cirrhosis, so it's pills and not a liver transplant for you."

"Maybe not pills either, not at that price."

"The University is still debating whether it will break the bank to provide Harvoni for all comers with Hep C, but the drug is available from overseas for a lot less."

"Even half price isn't going to help me."

"How about nine hundred dollars... total, for imported meds."

"How is it possible that a drug costs like a hundred times more here than somewhere else?"

"There are different laws in other countries, especially India, about which drugs are protected by patents. This one isn't, so Indian drug makers are licensed to produce generics of it, which cost a lot less."

"But I can't fly to India."

"They'll send the pills through the mail. Almost half of all new generics in the US come from India already."

"Well nine hundred dollars is doable, not easy but we can make it happen. So you think I should go that route, Doc?"

"You've got a lot better chance of a cure with an Indian generic drug, than waiting for who knows how long for the hospital to cough up ninety-four thousand dollars for each patient in the hepatitis clinic. Don't get me wrong. I think eventually they will decide that the pills are a smarter way to go than waiting until cirrhosis arrives and the only treatment is a liver transplant. Talk about high costs!"

"How much is a life worth?" asked Jorge.

"To me," said his wife, "yours is priceless."

CHAPTER 28

KEEPING COMPANY

"I know people don't get dressed up for the theater anymore, but I have to do what feels right. Call me old fashioned."

"Have it your way Dad. It's no big deal. The important thing is that you feel comfortable. Relax, it's going to be OK."

"It seems so foreign. I'm not sure I know the guy going out tonight. Most of all, I don't want to appear foolish, a fossil who doesn't believe the calendar."

"Dad, you taught me a long time ago not to put much weight in what others think of you as long as you are comfortable with your decisions. So get comfortable and get going before you're late. Speaking of which, I'd better get a move on; Roger will be here in thirty minutes. Gotta get beautiful."

"Me too, although I've got a lot less to work with," he said, his grin matching hers.

Doc stood for a long moment at Julia's door. It opened before he decided to knock.

"Thinking of running for the hills?" she said.

"No, and by the way you look lovely."

"You dress up pretty good yourself, Doc. Think the Broward Center is ready for two such elegant theatergoers?"

"Well, only one way to know." And off they went, opting for valet parking rather than the uphill walk from the adjacent parking deck. They picked up their tickets at 'Will Call' and then walked to a nearby restaurant where Julia had reserved a table, bypassed the waiting line and ordered quickly to avoid the pre-show rush.

"So I don't dominate the conversation, as I have been known to do," said Julia, "How about we reintroduce ourselves, one sentence at a time. I have some friends who tried this and it's really fun."

"OK, Ladies first."

"Ever the gentleman. I was born and raised in Allentown and went to the University of Pennsylvania; your turn."

"I'm a Brooklyn boy—Boy? Ha—and went through the New York school system, then to the Medical College of Virginia."

"I met my husband at Penn, we got married after graduation, I was a stay-at home Mom for three kids, eventually got a teaching license and taught fifth grade until we both retired nine years ago. See, I do tend to dominate the conversation. That's gotta be the longest sentence in the history of this game."

"That's pretty much my story as well. Roberta and I dated in college and got married after my first year in Medical School, against my parent's wishes."

"Didn't they like Roberta?"

"They didn't want to get to know her because then they would like her; isn't that weird? In their generation marriage was believed to take time from your studies and they were convinced that I would flunk out of med school. The joke is that being married made me so much happier, I studied better and my class standing improved." The dinner came, was eaten as the conversation continued, and Doc couldn't recall a single thing he ate at the end of the meal. He looked at his watch and both were surprised to see it was time to get to the theater. Doc paid saying "It's only right since you sprung for the theater tickets."

Julia seemed to know every fourth person in the lobby and introduced Doc, stating both names. He noted a very clever trick when she didn't appear to remember the person's name, saying "I'd like you to meet my friend Doc," leaving the person to introduce themselves.

"I once heard a comedian say that when you hit sixty-five the noun center of your brain dries up like a raisin. Mine must have shriveled long ago," said Julia. "One of my favorite writers Judith Viorst uses as her mantra, 'I knew it before, I'll know it again, I just don't know it right now.' The harder you reach for it, the word floats further away, just outside your grasp. Seems when you stop concentrating on it, your brain eventually pulls it out of the swamp."

Doc smiled the smile of recognition. "I imagine my brain as a beautiful research library with wooden shelves stretching to high ceilings, filled with memories; but the information has to be retrieved by a ninety-five year old librarian held upright by a walker."

"Compelling image," she said with a laugh, and Doc savored the warmth of her smile.

He didn't feel out of place being one of the few men wearing a sports jacket. He knew the standards of dress had changed but not the extent, with jeans and sneakers everywhere.

The seats were Right Orchestra and Doc made sure he took the seat furthest to the side. The musical, Waitress, was pleasant enough, if not memorable. Neither left the theater unhappy, nor humming a tune.

"I'd invite you in for coffee, but I don't want to scare you away."

"I don't scare easily, but I do have an early day tomorrow."

"I had a lovely evening Doc. You are such good company. I hope this wasn't too strange for you."

"I'd use a lot of words, but strange wouldn't be one of them. I haven't had this nice a time in years. I'd like to do it again."

"Soon," she added, as she gently kissed his cheek.

CHAPTER 29

THE MAGIC BULLET

"Hey Doc," said Marcey. "You're not going to believe this one. Your next patient is a lawyer."

"Are you trying to ruin my day before it even gets going?"

"This one is not a malpractice guy. He's a Public Defender."

"Well that's a first," said Doc as he headed to the waiting room.

"Hello, I'm Patrick Riley with the Public Defender's office. I know this may seem unusual, but I have a client who needs help and he has no money to hire a medical expert."

"Let me stop you right there. I don't claim to be a medical expert and I break out in hives at the thought of going to court."

"I understand, but what I need is a medical evaluation to give me a direction, to tell me if there is any reasonable defense."

"Well, maybe you'd best start at the beginning," said Doc as he led Mr. Riley to a more private space.

"My client, Henry Glass is a sixty-two year old truck driver. He was in an accident, others were injured and he was arrested for driving while intoxicated."

"Was he drunk?"

"Not this time."

"There were other times?"

"It seems Mr. Glass had a checkered past. He used to drink and had a series of DUI's in years past, two associated with property damage. But about a year ago he found AA when his wife threatened to leave, and both swear he hasn't had a drop since."

"Then why was he arrested?"

"The police said he had slurred speech and was unsteady when they did a roadside sobriety check."

"What about a breathalyzer?"

"They said theirs was broken, after his reading was negative."

"Was the accident his fault?"

"Oh, yes, no doubt about that. He went right through a red light and hit two cars in the intersection without slowing down. He's lucky he didn't kill anybody."

"And you want me to do what?"

"I would like you to come with me to the county jail, evaluate Mr. Glass, and tell me if there is any hope. If not, he stands to lose his license, his job and possibly his freedom."

"Whoa, that's a lot of responsibility to put on my shoulders. Tell you what I will do. I'll go with you tomorrow, but whatever I see—if it helps or hurts your client—I'll put in a report. You can use it or not, but I won't go to court."

"Deal. We can meet here at 10 tomorrow and drive down together."

They were cleared through the metal detectors and signed in. Henry Glass was brought to the interview room by a guard who told them he'd be right outside the door and with a steely look at Mr. Glass, said "Ten minutes and call if he gives you any trouble."

Mr. Riley introduced Doc and his client, a large man in need of a diet and some gym time. "Sorry we have to meet under these circumstances Mr. Glass."

"Please call me Henry, and thank you for coming all this way."

"First tell me what happened."

"That's it, I don't remember. I was making my deliveries as usual, and the next thing I know, smoke is coming out of my engine, the hood of my truck is up in the air like an elephant's trunk. Then the police are there pulling me out of the truck. They ran my license through their computer and that was it. They said I must have been drinking—I haven't had a drop since I joined AA eleven months ago. They said they smelled alcohol in the car, but that was just a bottle of Shalimar I bought for my wife's birthday. Who could smell alcohol over the vanilla scent anyway?"

"Your lawyer said you were a bit unsteady after the accident."

"True, but who wouldn't be. I was bruised and was trying to figure out what was going on. I asked to repeat the walking test after my head cleared and they said 'sorry, you're not going to be less drunk in five minutes'—I was not drinking."

"Any history of seizures, strokes, weakness on one side or the other?"

"None."

"Did you hit your head in the accident?"

"The air bag must have saved me from that. My face felt sore like I'd been hit with a boxing glove. It's just that I don't remember."

He continued to answer "No" to almost all questions. Doc especially probed cardiac symptoms, palpitations, blood pressure history, diabetes, sleep pattern– anything that might explain a brief loss of consciousness. He'd been eating well, maintaining his weight and had no symptoms suggesting liver disease, all seeming to support his claims of sobriety. The physical exam had just begun when the guard came in and said "Times up, This is an interview room, not the ER."

"But we just need a few more minutes," said the attorney.

"Let's go, rules are rules," said the guard. As he was being ushered from the room, Henry said over his shoulder, "There's one more thing. Just before the accident I remember that I couldn't see the right side mirror, as if it disappeared." With that he was ushered out of the interview room and out of sight.

"Any thoughts Doc?" asked the attorney.

"I don't see a smoking gun yet, but I need to think about this. Can I speak with his wife."

"Time is really of the essence. He will be arraigned Monday. If you can come up with something by then maybe we can talk with the ADA and get this dismissed. This poor guy can't afford bail, so I'm afraid he's stuck here till then."

Doc spoke with Mrs. Glass that afternoon.

"Has he had any passing out spells?"

"No, not since he stopped drinking."

"Are there times when he isn't there for a couple of minutes?"

"No, not that long."

"What do you mean not that long?"

"Well Henry does have times when he doesn't seem to be listening especially after dinner. We may be boring but we're certainly loud."

"One final question. Your husband said something about not being able to see the right sided mirror on his car. Has he ever complained of visual problems before?"

"Nothing that lasted a long time."

"Tell me about that."

"Well once or twice in the last month he asked me to look in his eye to see if there was something in it because he couldn't see out of it. Then it went back to normal in a couple of minutes and I didn't think more of it.'

"Do you remember which eye?"

"The right, both times it was the right eye, I'm sure."

"I think you just gave us the keys to his freedom," said Doc. "I just need to speak with his attorney."

"Mr. Riley, You have to get me in that jail again so I can complete my physical exam and I may have an answer for you."

That afternoon they found themselves waiting in the same interview room as Mr. Glass was led in by the same guard who glared at them and said "Ten minutes, not a second more."

"I won't need more than five," said Doc who took out his stethoscope and went straight for the patient's neck. Following habits long ingrained, Doc listened to the normal side first. The left carotid artery was unremarkable. Then he placed the stethoscope over the right carotid and knew he had the answer. The loud swishing sound of a severely narrowed vessel was unmistakable. "Henry, you have carotid stenosis, a marked narrowing of a main artery to the brain."

"So are you telling me you found the magic bullet?" said Mr. Riley.

"It looks like it," said Doc. "I think Henry didn't remember the accident for a very good reason; he was not conscious."

"How can he drive a car and not be conscious? Is he sleep walking?"

"I don't think so. A more likely cause is a carotid TIA."

"You mean a stroke?" asked Mr. Glass.

"Not in this case. A small blockage that resolves quickly, a TIA or transient ischemic attack, can explain all the symptoms. This can block circulation to the eye, causing temporary loss of vision, unsteady gate and even brief loss of consciousness."

"Henry, you were the one who gave me the critical piece of information, that you couldn't see the right sided mirror just before the accident. That happens when small pieces of material break off and go to the eye as well as the brain."

"Could this recur? Is he in any danger?" asked the attorney.

"Yes and yes. We need to get a carotid ultrasound done and get Mr. Glass to a vascular surgeon ASAP."

"The ADA is a friend of mine. Considering the urgent nature of Mr. Glass's condition. I think I can get this matter resolved today."

"Seems like *you* are the magic bullet Doc."

"Told you I would do most anything to avoid going to court."

CHAPTER 30

THE STORM

"It's coming Doc. This one is not going to catch the jet stream and head up north. Looks like a category 4 or even 5 and the clinic doesn't even have shutters. I've been on the phone with the County Emergency Manager's office. Sounds like organized chaos there and we're low priority since we're technically not a county facility. Our glass front won't last ten minutes in hurricane force winds."

"Well you and I aren't going up on ladders to board up the place even if we could find a piece of plywood. Any other ideas?"

I could ask Brent to come down and help but he's putting up shutters at his mother's house; and this is not a good time to alienate my future mother-in-law. I wish we had shutters for this place. When I was a kid people used to duct tape windows but all that did was make bigger pieces of broken glass. And it was almost impossible to get that sticky stuff off the unbroken panes after the storm."

"We do have one resource that others may not have," said Doc, "our patients. How about we split up the list and call anyone who is even vaguely related to the construction industry. I'm not above groveling."

Two Hours Later

"My ear hurts Doc, from all the excuses. Some are fleeing northward, some are busy trying to board up their businesses, or their kids houses, or moving their boats to safer mooring. I got several, 'I'll see what I can do' and a couple of 'If I finish in time,' but nothing we can rely on."

"I didn't do any better Marcey. I think it's time to make a plan. What do we have here that's got to be protected?"

"There are the medical records," said Marcey. "But those are backed up by the hospital's EMR system. Problem is, power could be out for a long time. I think we'd better backup our files on a disc and take the computers with us."

"Make that two. You take one home and I'll take the other. Also one of us has to take the EKG machine, blood pressure cuffs and ophthalmoscopes."

"Don't forget the samples." said Marcey. If the pharmacies are closed, that may be the only source of medicines for our folks– when and if we get to reopen."

"Let's each take a bunch of our suturing kits and tetanus vaccine. I have a strong feeling we're going to need both. By the way I hope you filled up with gas because the lines are horrendous, and don't forget cash, for your personal use," said Doc.

"Got both yesterday. My folks told me about Hurricane Andrew. When the electricity went out the gas pumps and banks shut down. I've told all my near term preggies to check into the hospital since something about the low barometric pressure seems to bring on labor, and even Fire Rescue isn't coming during a Cat 5."

"I keep feeling like there is something I'm forgetting."

"You know Doc, this may be the last day we work together in this little clinic of ours," said Marcey, stopping to swallow. "We may get blown away, and that would be sooo bad for everyone. But I want you to know, I've enjoyed every minute, and..."

"Easy young lady. We're not done yet."

They heard the trucks before seeing, each with two or three men, plywood, a tool box, and power saws connected to generators. Two, three, eventually four trucks each driven by a man with a smile and a nod. "Think we'd let you down? said Jorge Morales, his jaundice gone, Hep C in retreat with the medication Doc had helped him locate. Bill Williamson drove the next truck. "Bill, I appreciate the thought and I know your heart failure is better, but not better enough to get up on a ladder or be lifting plywood sheets."

"That's why I brought these two bulls along," he grinned, pointing to his two burly sons. The third and fourth truck drivers were new fathers who were quick to show Marcey pictures of the product of her prenatal care.

The men talked among themselves for a moment, then Bill told Doc: "We don't need four of us to board up the clinic, but the stores on each side share your roof. Jorge will board up your place with three quarter inch plywood—nothing is going through that. I'm going to ask your neighbors if we can board up their stores so you all don't get that roof blown into the next county. Tom and Jack are going to go to your homes and get the shutters up. I understand yours is on a canal and pretty exposed, Doc. They just need the addresses and to know that someone is home." The skilled men took less than an hour to board up front and back. With backup discs, the two portable computers and medical equipment filling their trunks, a grateful pair of health care providers headed home.

Doc received the same phone call as all of the other doctors in the area: The University Hospital needed physicians to spend the night there since no doctors were coming in once the winds began to roar. Doc called and was told by the administrator that he would be most welcome since most physicians were staying home with their families. The hospital needed someone to go floor to floor and handle "problems." Lots of specialists were opting not to do this since they hadn't seen a patient outside their specialty for years.

"What about my daughter?" asked Doc.

"We'll find a bed for her. There should be plenty of them since we're discharging anyone who is in stable condition. And lots of the nurses are bringing their kids. We've opened a whole wing for them."

"You know, my daughter is a teacher. I bet she would enjoy keeping a bunch of kids entertained and maybe improve their writing skills at the same time."

"Just come before the wind picks up."

"Don't worry; I don't want to ride out this storm on I-95."

"Dad, how did you get our shutters up, without me?"

"I had professional help from some of our grateful patients and their families. How would you like to ride out this storm in a huge strong concrete building, the hospital?"

"I wasn't going to say anything but I am nervous about being in our house in a category 5 storm. What would I do at the hospital."

"Oh I don't think you'll be bored."

Doc felt safer the minute he arrived. They took Suzie's car, loaded with the clinic's equipment and parked it in the well protected doctors' parking deck. He left his ten year old Camry in the carport half wishing it would blow away.

By 8 p.m. the winds had begun to howl, a pitch that intensified until it seemed there was a freight train about to enter Med-Surg 4, the floor to which he had been summoned. The patient had abdominal pain and his doctor was 'not available'. Doc first looked at his chart. He was surprised to see that all the notes were typed. Seems the hospital has a voice recognition system for all progress notes, but no one had given Doc an access code or instructions on how to use it. Well, they would just have to get by with his handwritten comments. He had to admit that the dictated notes were easier to read, but so much more voluminous. Seems many copied the previous notes, misspellings and all. This meant that each doctor assumed the one before had done a detailed exam, which may not have been the case.

This patient had undergone neck surgery for spinal stenosis. Other than a scary and brief post-op period where he couldn't move his arms, his recovery had been uneventful. Today he had developed low abdominal pain and the nurses were concerned that he might have diverticulitis which he had twice in the past. Other than this and some reflux there was no history of other abdominal problems. The chart had multiple specialists' notes from earlier in the morning with normal abdominal exams.

"Hello Mr. Wells, I'm covering for your Doctor who can't make it in. When did this pain start?"

"I've had some earlier today but it got much worse an hour ago."

"Put your finger on where it hurts the most." The patient pointed to the low abdomen in the midline. "Any nausea or vomiting?"

"No."

"Bowels moving?"

"This morning."

"How about urinating?"

"Small amounts, but I pee frequently, sometimes before I get to the urinal. "Doc went straight to the abdominal exam, gently feeling, beginning far away from the painful area. Liver, not enlarged, no pain with taking a deep breath with Doc's fingers below his right ribs, making gall bladder disease unlikely. No tenderness in the upper abdomen midline, making a stress ulcer, not uncommon after surgery, less likely. No tenderness in the flanks. A firmness met Doc's fingers as he approached the lower abdomen. He gently palpated and felt the outline of a mass extending like a pregnant uterus to the umbilicus.

"That's it," said Mr. Wells with a wince. Doc looked again at the 'I and O' chart. The patient was making urine but only 100cc at a time plus some incontinence. His IVs had been increased because of the low urine output, to treat possible dehydration.

"Is it diverticulitis again? Am I going to need belly surgery now? I don't know if I can take another surgery. Can't I have some more pain meds?"

"Let me do a quick test and then we should be able to make you feel better right away." Doc asked the nurse to get an ultrasound machine which showed a liquid filled mass holding about 1,000 cc's—a giant distended urinary bladder.

"You have urinary retention Mr. Wells, not uncommon after surgery in men your age and on all the pain meds you've needed. The nurse is getting the equipment to place a catheter and drain that fluid. It should give you immediate relief. We'll take it out a few hundred ccs at a time so we don't drop your blood pressure." Doc found the phones were working and called the neurosurgeon, an old friend, to tell him of the events.

"Not bad for a guy who hasn't stepped foot inside a hospital for five years. You ought to do this more often Doc."

"Once a hurricane is enough for me, thanks."

Then he wrote a detailed progress note, making it as legible as possible.

CHAPTER 31

AFTER THE STORM

It took Doc and Suzie an hour and a half to make the twenty minute drive home from the hospital. It was a slalom ride around fallen trees and wires, up on lawns, playing low speed chicken with other frustrated drivers on the light-less street corners. They saw the best and worst of humanity in those ninety minutes. One man had donned the oversized gloves worn at football stadiums, using them to be seen while standing in the middle of a busy street directing traffic. And then there was one man standing on his lawn in front of his house, which had been bisected by a fallen tree, who had a gun and threatened to shoot anyone who drove on his mangled lawn.

Doc drove by his own block twice before realizing that this nearly treeless, unmarked expanse was where he lived. Random destruction replaced his placid neighborhood. Some houses seemed no more, reduced to foundations and a few walls, often a bathroom, still standing. Some houses seemed untouched. He saw his house from half way down the block, with the automotive landmark– his ten year old Camry–parked out front, but no sign of the carport. The shutters were indented as if a baseball team had used them for backstops. They removed the shutters from the back door and entered the darkened house. Suzie had brought flashlights and they walked slowly room to room, noticing only one cracked window, its covering shutter dented inward at a near right angle. They were an island of preservation in a sea of devastation.

They removed the other shutters one at a time, with Suzie climbing on the step ladder to reach the top bolts. They noticed more details of their neighbors' houses. Those without shutters had perfect window frames with no glass. There was some very intact plywood on Doc's lawn. He then saw the shingles attached to the other side. This was his neighbor's roof! After an hour, the main windows were uncovered and the house brightened. Power existed only at the houses with portable generators and many of those were soon silenced as the gasoline supply dwindled. The local gas pumps, minus electricity were just so many Easter Island statues.

Some people wandered through the detritus of their neighborhood, helpless and unable to cope; and Doc and Suzie invited them in for a drink or some food from their freezer before it spoiled, cooked on the gas barbecue. "I can do better than this," thought Doc. He opened his garage door, moved the dented Camry to the sidewalk, and set up a table in the garage. On it he placed the suture kits, xylocaine, bandages, the bottles of tetanus vaccine and his blood pressure cuff. Suzie took a piece of cardboard, wrote in big black letters: 'First Aid Station' and taped it to the front of the table.

Over the next three days many of the main streets were cleared by FEMA crews. The birds were gone and the only sounds were the welcome drones of the chain saw. Doc had many visitors, some with foot lacerations from broken glass, some impaling themselves on exposed nails. Neighbors wanted their blood pressure checked since they had run out of medication or worried about stress related hypertension. Doc's biggest fear was realized on day three when Visqueen, the shiny blue plastic used to cover perforated roofs, began to appear. It kept most of the water out until roof repairs could be completed, but made a slippery slope out of an angled roof. Jack was the first of several men who fell. He was brought to Doc by his wife, who said: "He had no business on that roof. If he didn't catch himself on the gutter, he would have broken his neck."

"Did he hit his head?"

"No, thank goodness, but he did get a nasty gash on his arm and by the grace of God he landed on his feet."

"How do you feel?" asked Doc.

"Pretty damned lucky, a little bruised and cut up, but all things considered, like I won the Lotto."

Doc found no evidence of fractures, cleaned the wound, placed sixteen sutures and bandaged with sterile gauze. After a tetanus shot, instructions to get the sutures removed in five days, and a promise that he was not going back up on the roof, the neighbor was off.

Ted Frawley was not so lucky. Suzie had taught one of his daughters years ago and Hannah, his wife, always had a friendly smile for her. This day, the fifth after the storm, there was only a look of panic. "Doc, come quick, Ted has fallen off the roof." Doc walked as fast as he could down the street which was now lined with cut branches and tree trunks stacked four feet high. He found his neighbor sitting against the house—a good sign that he can sit, thought Doc.

"Ted, what happened?"

"I don't remember."

"Do you remember being on the roof?"

"I must have been, cause the visqueen is on it."

"Was he knocked out?" Doc asked Hannah.

"I heard the thump, what a sickening sound. Then I came out here and he was on the ground, bleeding from his head. He wouldn't answer me. I thought he was dead," she said with a sob. "Then after what seemed like forever he opened his eyes. I helped him sit up."

"Squeeze my hand," said Doc, offering first his right then his left." His left grip was noticeably weaker, as was his left leg. He knew Doc but not the Year, or the President.

"Hannah, do you have a cell phone that works; I understand that the system is up again."

"No but the Burtons do; they have a generator."

"Good, go over there and call Fire Rescue."

"What should I tell them?"

"Tell them about the fall and that he is weak on the left side. I'm concerned about a possible brain injury or bleed in his head."

"Oh my God."

"It's not for certain, but we need to have him checked out at the hospital ASAP."

On day six, most large streets were passable. Doc borrowed a cell phone and called Marcey.

"Time to see if the clinic is still standing?"

"Glad you got me today. I'm going to meet Jorge Morales there at two o'clock this afternoon. He can remove the plywood and help pick up the pieces."

"Think positively."

The drive to the clinic was less harrowing than returning home, but not by much. Now there were National Guard soldiers directing traffic, with the electric grid a distant memory. He arrived to find Jorge talking to Marcey in front of the plywood armor.

"Hey Doc, looks like you guys dodged a bullet."

"Thanks to you and the others."

"You did lose a few shingles but not enough to make it rain inside. The landlord will have to get it repaired when he can pin down a roofer, which is not going to be easy."

"Think we can peel back this banana and see what this storm left us, "said Marcey.

"Sure," said Jorge as with one hard blow of his hammer he dislodged the two by four which had become the hypotenuse of the triangle, wedged between the top of the plywood and the sidewalk. Next the four by eight rectangles of plywood came down. There was not a scratch on the glass windows. They opened the front door and were inside as Jorge and his helper loaded the plywood into their truck. Other than the dark, the clinic was as they had left it a week, a lifetime ago.

"Well Doc, looks like your neighbor, the Dollar Store, has a generator and is open for business. I think he owes us one for boarding up his windows," said Jorge. Taking a thick yellow electric cord from his truck he said: "I'm going to talk to him about letting us piggy back onto his generator." Ten minutes later the clinic lit up and it was daytime again. Doc and Marcey unloaded the medical equipment and computers, plugged them in and were never so happy to see electronic medical records before.

"We're in business Doc."

"Judging from what I've been seeing, we're going to be busy. One of my neighbors wound up with an epidural bleed and needed neurosurgery to drain it. I hear he's doing well."

"I had to set one guys leg," said Marcey. "Haven't done that since training."

"As Suzie and I realized, this storm brings out the best and worst in all of us. Let's hope the best prevails," said Doc as he posted a sign in the front window:

"OPEN 9 A.M. TOMORROW".

CHAPTER 32
DETECTIVE MARCEY

"Flu season must have come early, Doc."

"Are you seeing lots of kids with fever and aches, Marcey?"

"More this week than all of last month, and they all seem to be in one school district."

"A cluster, that is interesting. Where?"

"Seems all are from an apartment complex near 1-95; although they come from the lower, middle and high school."

"Lots of cough and congestion?" asked Doc.

"Not really. They come in with chills, fever, aching muscles and most have headaches."

"How long does all this last?"

"That's the funny thing, it's shorter than the flu, maybe two to five days then they're back to normal. I'm seeing several kids in the same family, so it seems pretty contagious."

"I haven't seen anything out of the ordinary with my patients," said Doc. Perhaps he spoke too soon.

Doc saw the patient slumped in the waiting room chair. The man in his sixties was red faced, sweating, and coughed repeatedly into his sleeve. Doc apologized to those who had come earlier, saying: "I'm sorry folks but this man looks quite ill and needs to be seen first. I would do the same for you. I'm sure you understand."

Doc asked questions as he held the man's elbow and guided him into the exam room, to a few grumbles from the other patients.

"Call me Doc. What's your name?" No answer. "When did this start?" No answer. "Any previous illnesses? Coughing?. What is the main thing bothering you now?"

"Too many questions; my brain is not working so well. I'm Tim, Tim Dougherty."

"Sorry, let me slow down a bit. Is anyone here with you?"

"My wife is at home babysitting our two grandkids; they've both got a fever." "When did your illness start?"

"I got sick about three days ago, just after the kids. I've been coughing like mad, and each time it feels like my head is going to explode."

"Are the kids having the same symptoms?"

"Not really. They aren't coughing at all, just the same fever and chills, and their heads hurt too. But they seem to be getting better. Today I had shaking all over and my wife said I felt really hot. My temp was 102 and a half this morning and she made me call in sick and come here. She said I'd just give this to everyone at work; and the building could survive without me for a day or two. I'm not sure she's right about that."

"What kind of work?"

"I'm the superintendent at the Lauderdale Heights Apartments. Everything seems to break down when I'm not there. I came for some antibiotics so I can keep my wife happy and then go back to work."

"Whoa there. Let me examine you and then we'll talk about treatment and work." Doc put his palm on the patient's forehead, an old habit, and felt the heat even before their skin made contact. The thermometer read 104, heart rate 55, blood pressure 128/76. Doc heard the crackles in the bases of both lungs. The abdomen was slightly swollen and mildly tender. "Any problem with your stomach?"

"Lots of diarrhea, and I'm not hungry. I can take Imodium and go to work, can't I?"

"I'm afraid that wouldn't be a smart thing to do. You have pneumonia Mr. Dougherty, in both lungs. This is a serious situation. You need to go to the hospital, now, for IV antibiotics and monitoring. I'm concerned that your heart rate is too slow for someone with a high fever like you have, and it will have to be watched closely."

"But, what about work?"

"You are a sick man. I'm not trying to scare you, but some people, even today, die of pneumonia. The best thing we can do to ensure that you get better is to start IV antibiotics as soon as possible." Tim admitted defeat but insisted on driving himself to the hospital, over Doc's objections.

Two other people came in with pneumonia and high fever over the next two days. Doc began calling other local practitioners and each had seen one or two of the same type of illness. The patients wound up in different hospitals, each nearest to their doctor's office.

"You know Doc, I've been looking into my mystery illness, and there is something strange."

"What's that Marcey?"

"Most of the kids live in the same area, the same housing complex."

"Now that is interesting. You say most?"

''Three of the kids live at least a mile away. I thought I was onto something, but it doesn't explain how those three caught this bug."

"You may still be on the right track."

"I think I'll call them back and ask about play dates or visiting anyone in the apartment complex," said Marcey.

"You're becoming an epidemiologist."

"Just a curious caregiver."

"Which building?" Doc asked. With the address in hand, Doc went back to his computer and looked up Tim Dougherty's address. He lived in the building next door, but worked at the address Marcey had recorded.

Doc felt a shiver, as if an electric circuit had been completed, which in a way, it had. He called the patient, who was improving on broad spectrum antibiotics, and was to be moved from the ICU today.

"Hi, this is Doc. I'm glad to hear things are going well. I have one question. Where do your grandkids live?"

"That's a strange question. Do you have to report this to the Housing Authority?"

"Just humor me."

"You know that being the building superintendent has its privileges. I got them the first vacancy in the building where I work. They moved in last month."

Marcey came in as Doc hung up the phone.

"Doc, you're not going to believe this but all three of the kids who didn't live in the building, have visited there for a birthday party or play date."

"Marcey, you are a genius. Mr. Dougherty works in that building."

"I've heard of sick building syndrome, but all the illnesses don't seem to be the same," said Marcey.

"I think you are absolutely right about this being related to one location.

The two different kinds of illnesses seem odd, but there is one circumstance that can explain it all.

First I've got to call the Health Department and make them aware of your discovery, then the hospital."

"Did we discover a new disease, 'Marcey and Doc's syndrome', ladies first of course?"

"Actually I think it already has a name, Legionnaires Disease," said Doc.

"But I never heard of Legionnaires Disease in kids."

"Kids get sick from inhaling the same organism that grows in stagnant water in the air conditioning system of large buildings, but don't develop pneumonia like adults. They get the illness you've been seeing, something called Pontiac Fever."

"What can the Health Department do other than making everyone move out?" said Marcey.

"People may have to leave temporarily, but the water tanks on the roofs should be treated to eliminate the bacteria growing there.

Who knew that in addition to your nurse practitioner's license, you'd also get a detective's badge?"

CHAPTER 33

ALL IN THE FAMILY

Doc was late. It was unusual for him and he hated it, especially since Julia was one of those waiting. Today's clinic was particularly busy. The last patient turned into an hour and a quarter marathon, and Doc was keeping three canasta players waiting.

The harried physician greeted them with as much apology as he could muster. They all understood, and Bill teased Doc about stopping into a bar for a couple of drinks before he could tolerate their company.

"OK, you want the details? I was heading for the door when a family came in and begged to be seen. They were originally from Haiti and had been working in the fields picking tomatoes. The mother had become ill about a week ago with nausea and vomiting, but she kept working; then yesterday she developed a temp of 103, chills and worsening abdominal pain. She is the reason they came in. Their thirteen year old son translated and he was wonderful, telling me the exact words but also what they really meant. When Mom said she had 'belly ache' he explained that it was so severe she would curl up in a ball and moan, like when she was in labor with his little sister.

Both husband and wife were tall and stick thin, neither looking well. Between coughs, the father would be talking in Creole to his son, who would then translate into English. The Mom had almost all the symptoms I asked about, from weight loss, to headache, to night sweats, to malaise. She hurt everywhere especially her abdomen. When I examined her, the inside of her eyelids were pale, meaning anemia. Her belly was a bit distended and tender. When I pushed and let up suddenly, she sat up like she'd been shot. All findings suggested peritonitis."

"Sounds like what I had when my appendix ruptured," said Bill. "That was nasty."

"You're right; it's a diffuse inflammation of the abdomen often caused by organ perforation or infection. I told them she must go to the hospital immediately to find out what was causing her illness and that she might need emergency surgery. The mom refused to move until her husband was seen. Seems he'd been coughing for months and losing weight, but he refused to take time off work to see a doctor. In addition to the chronic cough, which sometimes produced blood, he had no appetite and was wasting away. I heard some crackles in the chest, in the upper lungs. We did one of our not so great x-rays and it was undeniable."

"Pneumonia?" asked Helen.

"Scarring and cavities in the both upper lobes, tuberculosis most likely, which is not uncommon in people from Haiti. Could be caused by rarer infections like fungus, but putting two and two together I think both husband and wife have active TB, he of the lung and she of the peritoneum."

"What about the children?" asked Julia.

"They will have to be tested for TB and treated prophylactically until their skin test, blood or X-ray is shown to remain negative over time. Thank goodness we didn't have a waiting room full of patients or they all would have to be tested. Then it took some time to get an ambulance. The drivers weren't thrilled at transporting patients with acute TB. I also had to call the ER and give them a heads up, to place both patients in isolation rooms. Same for the kids."

"So this is my doctor's note as to why I'm late."

Julia asked: "What about you Doc? Are you afraid of coming down with TB?"

"I developed a positive skin test when I was an intern and took a year of prophylactic treatment. It's extremely unlikely that I can get active TB as long as my immune system holds out. I'm the least of the problems."

By the time Doc finished his tale, most other players were finishing their first hand and Doc's table had yet to shuffle the cards. "That's fascinating," said Julia, "but how did you know?"

"When you practice as long as I have you learn to recognize the various faces of normal. Then it's a brief step to spotting abnormal.Once you know that someone is really sick, the history and physical will point you in the right direction. After that, blood tests or the high priced tools like CT scans or MRIs fine tune the diagnosis, Does that make sense?" All agreed that it did and Bill finally dealt the cards.

Doc and Julia seeming to anticipate each other's moves. By the break they were ahead and by the end of the evening they had won handily, for the first time.

"Have you two been practicing?" said Helen.

"No but we do appear to be in sync," said Julia. Doc looked around, eyeing the refreshment table.

"Oh my goodness, I didn't even ask if you had time to get dinner," said Julia.

"Actually I'm starving," said Doc. "Did you notice me inhaling those cookies at break time?"

"Still hungry? I've got some left over Kung Pow chicken and fried rice at my place," said Julia.

"Just what I've been craving, if it's not too much trouble."

"You're never too much trouble Doc." He drove her home and waited in the kitchen while Julia set the table and heated up the leftovers, which filled the kitchen with a delightful smell. Perhaps the old saying was true, thought Doc: 'Hunger is the best sauce.' He found himself completely at ease. Conversation flowed as if he had known Julia all his life. They talked until 11, and then realized the hour.

"Your daughter must be worried."

"Actually she's out on a date herself, on a weeknight. Must be serious."

"Can I get you anything else?" asked Julia.

"I don't plan to be hungry for a week. I wonder why," he said, pointing to the empty take-out cartons.

"I'm sure it will return sooner than that." She slid her hand over his and let it linger.

"I make a breakfast quiche you won't want to miss."

"Let me call Suzie and tell her not to expect me," said Doc.

CHAPTER 34

MEDICAL ETHICS

"Hi Doc, This is Gloria Bowen the hospital administrator. We met at that raucous Board meeting a couple of months ago."

"Ah, Gloria, of course I remember. What can I do for you?"

"We need someone with a few grey hairs and common sense to chair our ethics committee. The committee meets only twice a year but is on call for situations that arise."

"I'm not sure I should be telling other doctors what to do, since I've been out of the trenches for half a decade," said Doc.

"You don't tell anyone what to do, just offer an opinion that may help guide their decisions and those of the patient's. It's often really helpful to both and also tends to point us, the administrators in the right direction."

"Can I try it out without making a firm commitment? I don't want to walk into a long term responsibility." "Give it a month or so. If it is not a good fit we'll let you go with no hard feelings."

"OK, but why do I feel like I'm taking the first step over the edge of a cliff."

"We provide parachutes if needed," she laughed.

The first call came two weeks later. Doc met the committee in the boardroom, notable for the fine woodwork and the giant wooden table that must seat thirty people. Their group of six was huddled in one corner. Besides Doc there was Dr. Joseph Sterling, who was both an oncologist and Chief of Medicine, Alice Summers the Chief of Nursing / Assistant Administrator, Carolyn Rice, head of the social work department, the chaplain and the hospital's attorney. Doc was surprised to see the attorney but then realized the legal implications of any issue and understood.

Alice Summers called the agenda after introductions all around.

"I guess you are the new chairman, Doc," said Dr. Sterling. "And good luck to you." Doc felt the spike buried in the well wishes and refused to react.

"It's like spring training. This is tryout time and I'm not sure if I'll make the team."

"Oh you are our #1 draft choice," was the chorus from the others.

Alice Summers began: "The patient who brought us together today is Hank Adams, Henry James Adams, our maintenance supervisor. Hank has been with the hospital since we moved into the new building nearly twenty-seven years ago. He was diagnosed with prostate cancer seven years ago. It was initially treated with robotic surgery, but the PSA began rising shortly thereafter and he was started on Lupron shots for hormone suppression. This kept the PSA's at barely measurable levels until two years ago when his bone scan turned positive in the pelvis and spine. Initially he was asymptomatic and his hormone blockade was stepped up with a second drug.

Recently he came in with severe back pain due to tumor spread to his L4 vertebra which had partially collapsed. He is refusing pain meds."

"Why?" asked Doc.

"He says it 'fogs my brain and makes me into a babbling idiot'," she read. He says he wants to die. Dr. Sterling's group is taking care of him, and they say that further treatment would help him.

Dr.Sterling: "I think it would be malpractice to give up on Hank at this point. He could benefit from chemo and also local radiation to ease his pain. I for one am not willing to write him a prescription for oxycontin and send him home. I'm not sure why this committee is discussing Hank. He needs treatment, plain and simple."

"Who made the referral to this committee?" asked Doc.

"I did," said the social worker. "Hank is requesting assistance to end his life."

"We don't do that in our state," said Dr. Sterling.

"But we do believe in comfort care and hospice," countered the social worker.

"Why does he want to stop care?" asked Doc.

"What difference does it make," said Dr. Sterling. "We didn't sanction mercy killing when I was chairman of this committee."

"We're not sanctioning anything, just making suggestions," said the chief of nursing. The hospital attorney nodded his agreement.

"I think we need to follow precedent here, and state law!" said Dr. Sterling.

The attorney began to quote state statutes and three conversations broke out at once.

"How about we all go and talk with the patient," said Doc. "It should be less threatening if I ask a few things first. If you still have issues at the end I promise you will have an opportunity to ask about them."

"Hello, Hank. Just call me Doc. I'm here with a group from a hospital ethics committee and we're trying to figure out the best way to help you."

"You could give me a handful of pills and stop wasting everyone's time."

"Talk to me about what you are feeling now."

"I'm feeling a lot of pain in my back that gets worse even when I put on socks, not to mention lifting the stuff a custodian has to drag around. I won't be one of those guys who sit in a recliner and moans."

"You've been active all your life?"

"You bet. I left home at 17, joined the Marines and have worked with my hands, like a man, ever since."

"This hormone blockade getting to you?"

"It doesn't help that I get night sweats, but not working, that's the worst."

"Would you feel differently if your pain went away?" said Doc.

"If it would stay away and the meds wouldn't fog up my head, then yeah, it would be a whole different story, but I see myself going downhill from here on out."

"You know that radiologists can insert a type of cement into the backbone to firm it up. It often takes the pain right away. Then we can get you some local radiation therapy which will give you even more relief."

"But, you need chemo," interjected Dr. Sterling. "to keep the tumor under control."

"I've seen what that stuff does to people," said Hank. "I don't want to be remembered as a walking cadaver."

"If you had no back pain, could you go back to work?"

"Sure, I'd jump at the chance to work again, if I only could."

"What about your family? What do they advise you to do?"

"My wife and son want me to take the chemo–why don't they just call it poison and be more honest."

"How about we take one step at a time and see if we can make you more comfortable. Then you can decide about chemotherapy. Your decision may be a bit different if you are not in constant pain. Also, it's natural to have feelings of depression when you are sick. Sometimes treatment for that can make a world of difference."

"I've been very down lately between worrying about my illness and how the family is going to get by without me."

"Let's not go down that alley, because as you know lots of forms of cancer can be controlled and treated like chronic medical illnesses. Any flare up is treated, like we're suggesting, then often patients are without symptoms for years," said Doc.

"Any other questions for us?"

"When can you get this back pain to go away so I can get back to work?"

"We'll recommend starting treatment ASAP." The committee had no further questions.

After the meeting

"Thanks Doc. You really did a good thing," said the social worker.

"Thanks Doc for helping us help an old friend," said the director of nursing.

"You made me look like a callous clod, and I won't forget that," said Dr. Sterling.

"How could I have forgotten about hospital politics?" thought Doc.

CHAPTER 35

FACE TO FACE

The following week, Doc awakened with an odd sensation in his mouth. It wasn't numbness, yet something felt out of kilter. He followed his well worn track to the bathroom more out of habit than conscious thought, picked up his toothbrush, and noted that the toothpaste had an off taste, like soap. Doc was instantly wide awake as he glared at the mirror and saw toothpaste and saliva dribbled down the sagging left side of his mouth.

His left hand opened and closed before he was aware that he had begun a self exam. He lifted his left leg, stood on the toes and heels and walked a few steps as the word "stroke" was entertained, then dismissed. He stared into the mirror to see a fun house distorted image of his face. Symmetry was gone; smiling caused a leer. His left eye wouldn't close on command, remaining half way open no matter how hard he tried. He touched both cheeks and there was no numbness. Doc saved the most definitive test for last. He tried to lift both eyebrows but only the right went up. He let out a sigh of relief, for he had ruled out a central neurologic event, a stroke, where the eyebrows would raise normally, leaving a self diagnosis of Bell's palsy.

Doubts reached high tide and flooded his brain. How could he function as a doctor with a drooping eye and mouth, blotting tears and saliva while trying to concentrate on someone else's problems? How could patients have confidence in an old, old man, now visibly deformed? How would Julia react now that he looked like something out of a horror movie?

After repeating his exam twice more to be sure, he called an old colleague—an infectious disease specialist–now retired and living in North Carolina.

"Hey Doc, Great to hear from you. The one thing I really miss in retirement is seeing you and the other guys in the doctor's dining room. Don't get me wrong, it's beautiful here and there's lots to do. Are you planning to come up here? It would be great to see you."

"I'd love to but this is a medical question."

"I should have known. I heard you are back in practice at the clinic. So tell me about your patient."

"Actually you know the patient quite well; it's me."

Doc could hear the change in his friend's tone from banter to 'doctor's voice'.

"Do tell."

Doc related his findings and the conclusion of Bell's palsy.

"Are you having pain behind your left ear?"

"That started yesterday. I didn't realize it was part of the syndrome."

"It is. Any sticking feeling in your eye?"

"Just a little."

"That often occurs because the eye doesn't close completely. You'll need to use artificial tears and a gel at night. Taping the lid closed when you sleep is helpful. Because Bell's palsy is related to the Herpes simplex virus attacking the facial nerve, we need to get you on high dose steroids, prednisone 60mg/ day for five days then taper. No one has demonstrated benefit from anti-virals but I doubt anyone has started them so soon." You've made the correct diagnosis and in record time.

"I'm game," said Doc. "As I recall, this can linger for weeks."

"Or months, but thanks to your quick diagnosis we have the advantage of starting treatment immediately," his friend added.

Doc thanked him and began the meds that day. Shortly after, he felt as if his mind was racing and yet clouded, as if he had had a couple of drinks. That Saturday he spent his time looking through the real estate ads, convinced that a condo in North Carolina would be the perfect antidote for Florida summers.

When he found one near his friend, Doc called him to get more information.

"Whoa, Doc. I would certainly like to have another friend up here but I'm sure you are aware what high dose steroids can do. I should have emphasized it."

"I know, you get a little speedy."

"More than that, your judgment is off, like someone in a manic episode."

"But it's such a good buy."

"I tell folks not to make any big decisions until you've tapered down below 20mg per day. So for now let's try separating the steroids into three doses. The condo isn't going away. We can revisit that issue when you are well."

Doc spent five nights engrossed in three a.m. infomercials, unable to sleep. He felt a need to move his limbs and a mind that jumped incessantly from politics to the North Carolina condo."

"This must be what meth addicts feel like," he said to himself before making a physical effort not to buy the currently featured product, a bottle of "second skin" which coats and seals any surface with a layer as thick and repellant as rubber. When they began with "and that's not all" he had to turn off the TV.

Doc thought long and hard about going back to the clinic.

"Marcey, I'm not sure I can trust my judgment."

"You are really needed here. The fact that you are doubting yourself tells me you will be extra careful, Doc.

How about if you see the patient and then we discuss it before the patient leaves, like a second opinion. We'll have a code word, say "steroid excess", if I disagree."

And so it went for a week, Doc beginning each visit with "No, this isn't my Halloween mask, my facial muscles have gone on vacation." After a question or two from the curious as to how long it would last and what it was called, patients seemed to relax and tell their stories more easily since illness was now a two way street.

At the end of five days Doc could see the beginnings of improvement. He still had to tape his eye closed at night but his mouth sagged less. By two weeks, he could lift both eyebrows enough so a stranger would not have looked twice. By three weeks he was back to normal in muscle strength and sleep. He no longer watched TV at three a.m. and could sleep through the night.

Julia had been a champion throughout. It helped that she had had Bell's palsy in high school and it lasted for two months. "Doc, I love that you face the issue head on with your patients and get it out of the way. I was so self conscious that I covered the mirrors in my bathroom the whole time. I think it's amazing that you can work while taking all that medication and you can still play an expert game of canasta."

If there had been any doubts they were now erased.

Doc knew for sure that she was a keeper.

CHAPTER 36
TO CHOOSE

Doc sat in his office and pondered the word 'Choose.' Such a simple word. In his youth it meant choosing sides for a stick ball game by calling odds or evens, counting 'one, two, three, shoot' and then putting out one or two fingers. If you won you got to select the best hitter or pitcher available; or if you were like Doc, you chose your friend Barry whose humor and razor sharp insights about teachers made up for a lack of coordination when the rubber ball was fired at the rectangular strike zone.

What had Doc's life been if not a series of choices: to go to college or work and help out with the family's rent payment; to continue on to med school; whom to have as a partner for the rest of his days, sleep with, have children with, choose with. Now he had a new set of choices. His wife of so many years was gone and he had finally met Julia, someone with whom he could share his remaining years. Would it be disloyal to his wife's memory? He thought not. His daughter told him it would not, but still there was a lingering discomfort, almost physical, that he felt at times of indecision.

Doc was good at compartmentalizing, which usually meant leaving the office problems at the office. Now it was the opposite, with personal decisions intruding on his consciousness at work—and he needed to concentrate. He had a patient, Barry's son Evan, who had been given one of the shortest straws in life. In his late thirties he had come to Doc, not one of the fancy downtown offices, when abdominal pain visited and wouldn't leave. Doc felt the lumps, hard and attached where none should be. He ordered the scans, chose the best surgeons and the most skilled and compassionate oncologist when unresectable colon cancer was discovered. Doc felt each deteriorating lab result like a blow, one from which he could not shield his old friend. This was never easy, but a man so young who had recently married and hadn't had time to start a family, a man so endlessly optimistic? All reasonable chemotherapy had been tried; some drug trials so experimental that even the correct dosage had yet to be established. Doc could see his patient's will eroding as if each piece of bad news consumed what optimism remained.

Doc slept less well, though often beside Julia. She thought their new relationship was interfering with his sleep and eventually tip toed into that territory. Doc owned up to certain feelings of guilt despite Julia echoing his daughter's phrase: 'People need people.' How many times had he told patients that those who live alone, in his experience, don't live as long or as well? Finally he told her of the young man's suffering and the terrible choice facing him: to abandon active treatment and begin Hospice care, or to continue to chase the vanishing vision of a cure. Evan had relied heavily on Doc for advice and was doing so now. Doc was not sure he was up to the task. Should he encourage Hospice, a decision that was becoming more acceptable to the patient with each pound of weight loss, each unbidden cramp, a decision that Barry had until now, strongly opposed.

"Doc, you can always confide in me," said a relieved Julia. "I know about all the HIPAA regulations and would never, never utter a word about any of your patients, even though the rules seem so perverse. You bear this burden, which is intruding on your sleep and yet you are not able to share it. It can't be good for your health."

The next day Doc set up a bedside conference, for the young patient had once again been admitted for pain relief. Evan's wife, Barry and the oncologist were also there. "It's time to choose, that powerful yet awful word," said Doc. "We can offer advice and love and what information we have. Only you know how terribly you are suffering. Chemotherapy hasn't worked. As your oncologist has said, there is no new treatment on the horizon. It hurts us all to see you suffer like this, Evan, but ultimately you must choose. The Hospice nurse has told you what they have to offer. If you choose that road you must then decide when to start. I'm so sorry to say that it is not a question of whether your life will end but when and under what circumstances. You must choose, or the tumor will choose for you."

The young man eventually elected Hospice care and lasted two weeks, much of which was spent in and out of sleep with enough awake time to hug, to say what needed to be said, to give his wife permission to go on.

Doc stood at Barry's side at the funeral, their tears mixing in the red dirt they shoveled on the polished wooden coffin. Though deeply saddened, everyone had slept better after the bedside conference. Evan had regained a measure of control over his remaining life. The wall of indecision had been surmounted. As Doc knew, the hardest part was choosing.

As far as his relationship with Julia, Doc had chosen.

CHAPTER 37
WEDDING SURPRISE

"No jugglers Julia, that's my only requirement. I don't want to look foolish."

"Relax Doc; ours is a plain old wedding at home with the vows administered by my nephew. He's a notary and to be certain he just became licensed by some Universal internet church–don't ask–but it is legal, I checked. I've already had the big affair fifty years ago and I suspect you have too. Besides, it's just too much work to do that again. Remember: you couldn't seat this cousin with that uncle because they were still feuding over a ten year old snub. And who needs to worry about whether an ice sculpture will melt if the ceremony goes on too long. Simple is the word of the day, and uncomplicated."

"Dignified is not a bad word either. I think my blue suit qualifies," said Doc.

"So does my red dress; ivory seems too obvious."

"Well I guess it really doesn't matter. I could wear a bowling shirt and we'd still be married," said Doc.

"As long as it doesn't clash with my red dress." Both laughed.

Suzie came down and did some last minute arranging. "Well Dad, are you ready?"

"Are you? To give away your Dad?"

"I'll never give you away. You're a keeper. By the way, our roles may be reversed soon. Things are going very well with Roger."

"Let's not rush this one."

"I hear you," said Suzie. "Don't worry. We won't jump up and make this a double wedding....although...."

Doc glared at her, or at least pretended to before breaking into a big grin.

The doorbell rang and Suzie was the first to open it and see the floral delivery driver, a woman in her forties, leaning on one doorpost, a bouquet of flowers beginning to slip from her hands. Suzie grabbed the flowers and the woman's arm in one deft move and guided her to the sofa.

"Dad! I need you in the living room, NOW," she called. Doc came through the kitchen door and helped control the woman's collapse onto the couch. He gently laid her down. She immediately began apologizing and Doc interrupted: "No need for that. I'm a doctor. Let me ask a few questions. Has this ever happened before?"

"Not any time recently."

"You look quite pale," said Doc as he inverted her eyelid which was white as the table cloth. The color of her cheeks was not all that different. "Have you had dizziness with standing?" asked Doc.

"Just in the last couple of days."

"Any bleeding, heavy periods, black stools?"

"No, no and no," she answered slowly.

"Any history of anemia?"

"Well, they did say I was anemic with my pregnancy, and they gave me some iron pills that made me constipated. I never followed up with the specialist, like they suggested. I didn't have insurance and couldn't afford it. They cost a fortune, and all those lab tests would wipe out our savings."

All the while Doc held her wrist and checked her pulse, noting that it was slowing from the original count of 120/minute. "Any family history of anemia?"

"My mother and grandmother were both anemic, but it was no big deal. They lived into their 80's. My Mom did have two babies that died."

"Take any new meds recently, especially antibiotics?"

"No."

"Here's a really strange question? Eat any new foods lately."

"Well we did go to a new Italian restaurant and tried all kinds of new stuff."

"Any with beans?"

"Yeah, some kind of beans, I remember the name because Hannibal Lechter, that creepy movie serial killer, told Jodie Foster about them."

"Fava beans?"

"Yeah that's it."

She called the floral shop owners who were very understanding, and promised to send a substitute driver to pick up the truck within the next two hours. "No, no ambulance, Doc," she insisted. "It will make too much of a fuss, especially with your guests coming; besides I'm feeling better." She called her husband to pick her up. He too was on a delivery but would head over as soon as possible.

"What happened to me?"

"It will take some more testing, but I think you may have a disease called hemolytic anemia where many of your red blood cells break apart."

"Why would it come out of the blue? I felt great a week ago."

"I suspect it's caused by an enzyme deficiency, called G6PD deficiency, that you have had your whole life. It doesn't present a problem unless you are exposed to certain drugs like those containing sulfa or foods that may make many of your red cells fragment. One of those foods is fava beans.

We can have you stay here for a little while but when your husband arrives you'll have to go to the hospital.

In the meantime, you need to hydrate to help your kidneys clear some of the hemoglobin floating around from the injured red cells. So grab a glass of water and keep drinking."

"Well Julia, I guess we'll have one more guest at the wedding," said Doc.

"I always wanted a flower girl," said Julia. "She's a little older than I envisioned..."

"But then so are we," said Doc, finishing her sentence.

"At least we don't have..." said Doc,

"Jugglers," said Julia.

CHAPTER 38

REUNION

It was 5:30 a.m. and Julia could sense Doc's absence. She felt his side of the bed, flat, though the wrinkled sheets were still warm. She put on her robe, the pink one she'd bought for their honeymoon and worn only twice in the two months since, slipped into her Uggs, the world's most comfortable slippers, and went in search of her wandering man.

She found Doc pacing in his den, far enough away not to disturb her.

"Damn, did I wake you again?" asked Doc.

"I missed your warmth. Any second thoughts about having remarried, Doc?"

"Oh, no, no, no, no,"

"So that would be a no."

"That would be a very strong no."

"Then what, is something hurting you?"

"Only my heart."

"Something I..."

"NO, NO, NO," he interrupted, then smiled and added, "That would be a definite no. It's the reunion, my fiftieth medical school reunion. I've been writing to a half dozen members of our class, encouraging them to come and have been getting some pretty disturbing responses. Now I don't know if I even want to attend."

"What kind of responses?"

"I just heard that Will Davidoff had a stroke, five years ago, and is in a wheelchair. He's not sure he can get his aide to make the trip. Can you imagine having to travel with as much paraphernalia as we used to drag along when we took an infant to see their grandparents? Going through metal detectors at the airport, pat downs, so humiliating."

"What's really bothering you honey?"

"What kind of friend am I that I didn't even know he had a stroke? And his wife, Ellen, had lots of trouble finding words. But there was something about her speech that was more than just the usual. She had a clipped, soft speech that sometimes ran on. I'll bet she's developing Parkinson's."

"So you are making over the phone diagnosis in addition to everything else? No wonder you can't sleep. Do you think you have had a few things on your plate, with losing your wife, jumping in to help at the free clinic, not to mention me? I'm sure your classmates were in the same boat. I suspect Will couldn't call you either."

"I didn't even think to invite them to our wedding."

"Now that is not reasonable, Doc. We both agreed to keep it small. There was no room in my house for another soul."

"And that's not all. There are seventeen names on the class list that say only 'deceased.' I don't even know what happened to them, what was their dash?"

"Their dash? Now you've lost me Doc."

"It's an old expression when you look at a tombstone: it's not the years of birth and death that really matter, but what they did with the dash between those two dates."

"We all drift apart Doc, even our own families. We get enmeshed with the everyday nets that snag our time. Our calendars move more quickly when we're tied up with little tasks. Only at punctuation points, like reunions and funerals, do we look at the big picture and talk about how time has slipped away."

"I've been fortunate. I still have my memory intact—other than the nouns, which seem to be just out of reach—and my body has held up as well as can be expected. I just feel so guilty," said Doc.

"Hold on here. Aren't you the one who told me that guilt was the permanent pallbearer at every funeral? Do I have to remind you that everyone thinks they could have done more, feels they should have done more?"

"You never cease to amaze me Julia. If I knew you were that smart I'd have married you a lot sooner."

"Part of brilliance is keeping it to yourself. Now let's get on line and book some tickets to this reunion so I can meet those of your classmates with enough courage to show up and put their best face forward."

CHAPTER 39

ANNIVERSARY

Doc and Julia celebrated their first anniversary in the warmth of friends and family. Bill and Helen were there, as were Marcey and Brent, she back from maternity leave and of course Suzie and her husband Roger, soon to celebrate their first anniversary. It was an evening of catered ease and conversation, lots of laughter and reminiscence. They joked about how hard it was to get Doc to accept that first canasta game and how they knew it had been the right thing to do before the end of that night. No one laughed more than Julia, who relived their shared reluctance to date after so many years. "That was the best evening that almost never was," she said. "I nearly backed out twice."

"I'm so grateful that you didn't," said Doc, sliding his hand over hers and lingering in each other's gaze, a moment that brought smiles around the room.

"Well Doc, now that I'm back and the residents from the med school are still available to help, you can cut back to three days a week if you want," said Marcey.

"This daily routine is wearing, though it feels good, knowing what's going on all the time," said Doc. "Though, sleeping late a couple of days a week won't be a bad thing."

"So Julia, How is married life treating you? Is it what you expected?" asked Helen.

"So much better in a hundred unexpected ways, all wonderful, with one small exception..."

"That must be my kidney stone," said Doc.

"Well it was an uninvited guest on our honeymoon cruise," said Julia.

"You mean our almost cruise. I still owe you another one."

"The only thing you owe me is to stay healthy."

"It was pretty lucky Dad, the way it caused back pain just as you were about to board the ship," said Suzie.

"I'm not sure anyone who has been down this road would call having a kidney stone lucky. They did a great job in the Seattle hospital, finding a stone too big to pass and breaking it up with a laser."

"I still feel guilty about that," said Julia.

"Come on," said Doc. "Neither of us knew that almonds and spinach can cause kidney stones."

"I shudder to think that I was encouraging you to drink almond milk, and making my old standby, spinach salad, sure that they were healthier."

"It was a useful, if painful lesson that I remember to tell my patients: stones are most often calcium oxalate and the two easiest ways to elevate oxalate are to eat your favorite foods, almonds and spinach."

"How did that work out?" said Bill, pointing to the picture of Doc's 50th class reunion, on the end table.

"Couldn't have been better. I'm so glad Julia insisted we attend. Forty classmates showed up including my old friend Will Davidoff." Doc pointed to the picture of Will who was grinning from ear to ear, and had insisted on standing for the picture, using a cane.

They had vowed to FaceTime regularly and had met for dinner, on line, on the first of each month. Doc smiled at the thought of speaking with Will Davidoff's wife Helen, whose dentures had been replaced by dental implants and as if by magic her speech returned to normal, so no Parkinson's. Doc had Introduced Julia, to warm greetings by all. Many of his classmates were into their second marriages, which to Doc's surprise, were now of 25+ years duration. Several were still practicing and vowing to take their last breath in the office. Others had pursued different directions. One had studied finance and now taught personal financial management to high school students. One loved race cars, bought one and was restoring it to its previous glory. One was devoted to his golf game though no longer convinced that he could make the senior tour; but now was dedicated to playing every major links course, the theme of his vacation schedule.

Doc and Julia were comfortable in their new home, which included a great room for evenings such as this one. Both felt it would feel like less of an intrusion if they started life together in a new home. They would never forget their previous existence but were eternally grateful for this second act. They would not be moving from their former lives, but creating a new one together.

The evening had to end early for they both had to pack. Nothing was going to keep them from turning a missed honeymoon into an anniversary cruise.

For Doc and Julia it was a perfect evening. There were no disruptions with illness, no sick patients, no allergic reactions, just a man and his wife celebrating a sweet new life together.

Paul M. Gustman M.D., like Doc, grew up in Brooklyn, New York before attending and interning at the Medical College of Virginia. For several years he worked and taught family medicine residents at a Community Clinic. He went on to practice pulmonary medicine and critical care medicine for thirty-eight years in Miami, Florida.

After retiring in 2013, Dr.Gustman began studying writing at the Osher Lifelong Learning Institute of the University of Miami and is now an award winning essayist.

He has been married to his wife (and editor) Marilyn for fifty-four years and has two children and six grandchildren.

This is his second book and the first work of fiction. The first book, "Life's Lessons, prn" was a memoir.